Suddenly, audible ev   ...   ...of
the fire, there was a star...   ...k! Seiko,
who had been sagging in   ...us, stood erect.
Her wrists, which had been tied behind her back,
were already free, the flames having burned away
the rope. But even if this had not been the case it
would not have mattered. The strength that she
now exerted to snap the chains would have been
more than enough to break mere vegetable fiber.
As she stood there, ridding herself of the last of
her bonds, the crumbling remnants of her clothing
fell from around her smoke-smudged body. She
was like, thought Grimes, Aphrodite rising from
the sea—a sea of fire. And he, even at this moment,
had to repress a giggle. A Venus without arms, a
Venus de Milo, he might accept—but a bald-
headed one was altogether too much. (Her body
paint had survived the fire although her wig had
not.) Even so, she was beautiful—and her escape
from the pyre had brought a renewal of hope....

PUBLISHER'S NOTE

It is ironic that "Jack" Chandler dedicated this novel to his "favorite wrist watch" for he could not have known that his own time was fast running out. He died in June, 1984, shortly after mailing the manuscript of The Wild Ones to his literary agents in America, though he had apparently been in good spirits during its writing. It is therefore his very last novel, and, although some small parts of the long career of John Grimes, from ensign to commodore of the Rim Worlds, have not been filled in, it must conclude the multifold saga of that amazing career.

A. Bertram Chandler, born in 1912, paralleled that career in a terrestrial way. Starting as a merchant seaman, he rose to be captain of his own vessel plying the world's rim between Australia and New Zealand. An Australian by choice, he was considered the top SF writer of that land and was a winner of its leading SF Award, the Ditmar.

The novel he considered his masterwork, Kelly Country, an exciting concept of an Australia that might have been if history had worked out differently, will be published by DAW Books later in 1985.

THE
WILD ONES

A. Bertram Chandler

DAW BOOKS, INC.
DONALD A. WOLLHEIM, PUBLISHER

1633 Broadway, New York, NY 10019

DEDICATION:
To my favorite wrist watch.

DAW Collector's Book No. 623

First Printing, April 1985

1 2 3 4 5 6 7 8 9

PRINTED IN U.S.A.

Chapter 1

Sister Sue, John Grimes commanding, had made a relatively uneventful voyage from New Sparta to Earth and was now berthed at Port Woomera. But nobody seemed to be in a hurry to take delivery of her cargo, a quite large consignment of the spices for which New Sparta had become famous among Terran gourmets. This didn't worry Grimes much. His ship, of which he was owner as well as master, was on time charter to the Interstellar Transport Commission and until her holds were empty she would remain on pay. What did worry Grimes was that the charter had expired and that the Commission had indicated that it might not be renewed. Another cause for worry was that Billy Williams, his chief officer for many years

and, for quite a while, during the term of Grimes'
appointment as governor for Liberia, relieving
master, was taking a long overdue spell of planet
leave, returning to his home world, Austral. With
him had gone the Purser/Catering Officer Magda
Granadu, leaving Grimes with a shipful of com-
parative strangers, young men and women who
had not been among her complement when he
had first commissioned her. So he had to find a
replacement for Magda and one for Billy Williams.
The second officer, young Kershaw, was, in Grimes'
opinion, too inexperienced a spaceman for promo-
tion. It would be many years before he would be
capable of acting as a reliable second in command.

Meanwhile Grimes had no option but to hang
around the ship like a bad smell. Until he had
seen which ways the many cats were going to
jump he could not afford to leave her in the
fumbling hands of young Kershaw. And he wanted,
badly, to get away himself for at least a few days,
to revisit his parents' home in Alice Springs. The
old man was getting on now, although still churn-
ing out his historical novels. And his mother,
Matilda, although one of those apparently ageless
women, blessed at birth with a good bone structure,
would be wanting to hear a first hand account of
her son's adventures as governor of Liberia and
then on New Sparta.

He was beginning to wonder if he should make
the not too long walk from the commercial space-

port to the Survey Service Base, there to pay a courtesy call on Rear Admiral Damien. Even though not many people knew that Grimes was back in the Service with the rank of captain on the reserve list, everybody knew that he was an ex-Survey Service regular officer and that at one stage of his career his superior had been Damien, then Commodore Damien, who had been Officer Commanding Couriers at the Linisfarne Base. (But it was also common knowledge that young Grimes, as a courier captain, had been Damien's *bête noir*.)

Still, Damien owed him something. He had acted as the Rear Admiral's cat's paw during the El Doradan piracy affair, and on Liberia and, most recently, on New Sparta. The Survey Service pulled heavy Gs with the Interstellar Transport Commission. If Damien dropped a few hints in the right quarters the Commission would either renew the New Sparta time charter or find some other lucrative employment for *Sister Sue*.

So, after a not very satisfactory breakfast—the temporary, in-port-duties-only catering officer thought it beneath her dignity to cater to the captain's personal tastes and could murder even so simple a dish as eggs and bacon—Grimes got dressed in his best uniform, his own uniform with the Far Traveler Couriers cap badge and crested buttons. Then he sent for the second officer.

He said, "I shall be going ashore for a while, Mr. Kershaw. Should anything crop up I shall be with Rear Admiral Damien, at the Base."

The lanky, sullen young man with the overly long hair asked, "Is there any word, sir, about a replacement for Mr. Williams? After all, I'm doing chief officer's duties and only getting second's pay . . ."

I'm *doing the chief officer's duties*, thought Grimes indignantly. But he said, "The Astronauts' Guild have the matter in hand. As you know, I require Master Astronaut's qualifications for my chief officer. Unluckily you have only a First Mate's certificate."

Kershaw flushed. He knew that Grimes knew that he had already sat twice for his Master's ticket and failed dismally each time. He decided to drop the subject.

"When will you be back, sir?"

"That all depends upon the Rear Admiral. He might invite me to lunch, although that's unlikely. Or I might run into some old shipmates at the Base."

"It's a pity that you ever left the Service, sir," almost sneered Kershaw.

"Isn't it?" said Grimes cheerfully.

He walked down the ramp from the after airlock, puffing his foul pipe. The morning was fine although, with a southerly breeze straight from the Antarctic, quite cool. There were only a few ships in port—two of the Commission's Epsilon Class tramps (*Sister Sue* had started her working life as one such), a somewhat larger Dog Star Line freighter and, gleaming like a huge, metallic skep in the bright sunlight, some of the bee people who were her crew flying lazily about her, a Shaara vessel. (*Those bastards are getting everywhere these days,* thought Grimes disapprovingly. Once he had quite liked the Shaara but various events had caused him to change his attitude.)

All these ships, he saw, were working cargo. They all had gainful employment. His *Sister Sue* did not.

He identified himself to the marine guard at the main gate to the Base, was admitted without question. (Fame, or notoriety, had its advantages.) He looked with rather wistful interest at the Survey Service ships in their berths. There were two Serpent Class couriers, the so-called "flying darning needles." Grimes' first command—how many years ago?—had been one of these little ships. There was a Star Class destroyer. There was a cartographic ship, similar to *Discovery*, the mutiny aboard which vessel had been the main cause of his somewhat hasty resignation from the Survey Service.

But he hadn't come here to take a leisurely stroll down memory lane. He had come here to confront Rear Admiral Damien, to make a more or less formal request that this gentleman use his influence to obtain further employment, preferably another time charter, for *Sister Sue*. After all he, Grimes, was useful to the Survey Service even though very few people knew that he was back in their employ. And surely a willing—well, for some of the time—laborer was worthy of his hire.

He approached the main office block, passed another marine sentry. He went to the receptionist's desk where a smart little female ensign was on duty. The girl looked at him curiously, noting the details of his uniform. Obviously she was not one of those who knew Grimes by name and reputation. But she was young, young. There may have been giants in those days, the days when Grimes himself was young, but this pert wench would never have heard of them. (Yet. But legends persist and, almost certainly, there would be those on the Base who would be happy to regale her with all sorts of tales, true, half-true and untrue, about that notorious misfit John Grimes.)

"Sir?" she asked politely.

"Could I see Admiral Damien, please?"

"Is he expecting you, sir?"

"No. But he'll see me."

"Whom shall I say is calling?"

"John Grimes. Captain John Grimes."

"Wait, please, Captain Grimes."

She pressed buttons and the little screen of her telephone console came alive. Grimes shifted position so he could look over the ensign's shoulder. He saw Damien's face—that prominent nose, the thin lips, the yellowish skin stretched taut over sharp bones—take form. *Old Skull Face never changes*, he thought. And Damien could see him in his own screen, standing behind the girl. There was a flicker of recognition in the cold, gray eyes.

"Admiral, sir," said the girl, "there is a . . ."

"I know, Ms. Pemberthy. There is a Captain Grimes to see me. Or a Commodore Grimes. Or His ex-Excellency ex-Governor Grimes . . . All right, Grimes. I was wondering when you would condescend to come and see me. You know where I live. I'm still in the office where you were debriefed after you came in from New Sparta—when was it, now? three months ago?—and now you're back from New Sparta again. But you won't be going back there for quite a while, if ever. . . . As you know full well I always keep my finger on the pulse of things." Then, to the girl, "That's all, Ms. Pemberthy. Captain Grimes can find his own way up. He has only to follow the signs. Even Blind Freddy and his dog could do that much."

The screen went blank.

The girl turned to stare at Grimes.

"The admiral seems to know you, sir. But what is your rank, captain or commodore? And *are* you an Excellency?"

"I was," Grimes told her. "And I was, at one time, commodore of a squadron of privateers . . ."

"Privateers, sir? Aren't they some sort of pirates?"

"No," Grimes told her firmly.

Chapter 2

Damien did Grimes the honor of getting up from behind his huge desk, walking around the massive piece of furniture and advancing on Grimes with bony right hand outstretched. Grimes did Damien the honor of saluting quite smartly before shaking hands with the rear admiral. Damien motioned Grimes to a quite comfortable armchair before resuming his own seat. He put his elbows on the surface of the desk, made a steeple of the skeletal fingers of both hands and resting his chin upon the apex, looked intently at the younger man.

"Well, young Grimes," he said at last, "what can I do you for?"

"I do not think," replied Grimes, "that that was an unintentional slip of the tongue."

"Too right it wasn't. Nonetheless I may be in a position to do something for you."

"At a price, no doubt. Sir. How many pounds of flesh, or is it just my soul you're after?"

"Grimes, Grimes. . . . This uppity attitude does not become you. And I would remind you that you hold a Survey Service commission, albeit on the Reserve List. You are subject to Service discipline—and, when you are recalled to active duty, are entitled to the full pay and allowances for your rank in addition to the quite—indeed overly—generous retaining fee of which you are already in receipt."

Grimes' prominent ears reddened but he kept his temper. After all he had the services of himself and his ship to sell—and this was a buyer's market. He could not afford to antagonize Damien.

"And now, Grimes, what exactly are your current troubles?"

"Well, sir, I was hoping that the Interstellar Transport Commission would renew or extend my time charter on the Earth/New Sparta run. After all, my ship has given very good service on that trade. . . ."

"But not with you in command of her, Grimes, until recently. As far as New Sparta is concerned you're too much of a catalyst. Things have a habit of happening around you rather than to you. . . ."

"Mphm!" grunted Grimes indignantly.

"I wish that you'd break yourself of that disgust-

ing habit," said Damien. "I've told you before
that I do not expect naval officers to make noises
like refugees from a pig sty. But, to revert to New
Sparta, it will be better for all concerned if things
are allowed to settle down. Your boozing pal
Brasidus is doing quite well now that he no longer
has Queen Elena to stick her tits into everything.
Our Commander Lazenby is maintaining a watching brief, as I am sure that you know. You and
she are old friends, aren't you? And that obnoxious news hen Fenella Pruin has taken flight to
some other planet to do her muckraking. . . ."

"So you persuaded the Commission not to renew the charter," said Grimes.

"Hinted, just hinted. And I also hinted that
there was no need to bust a gut to get your inward cargo discharged. Until it's out you're still
on hire. And money, I need hardly remind you, is
money. . . ."

"Thank you, sir. And I wonder if you'd mind
hinting to the Astronauts' Guild that I have a
vacancy for a chief officer, one with some experience and with a master's ticket. Come to that, I
also want a new catering officer. . . ."

"Don't get your knickers in a twist, Grimes.
You'll be getting your new chief officer shortly.
One of our people, needless to say. And a very
good catering officer. And . . ." A sardonic grin
appeared briefly on Damien's face.

"And what? Or whom?"

"You remember Shirl and Darleen, the two young ladies whom you brought to Earth, as passengers, from New Sparta. . . ."

"How could I forget them?"

"Like that, was it?"

Again Grimes' prominent ears flushed angrily.

He said, "So it was you who arranged for their passage, in my ship, from New Sparta to Earth. Oh, well, as long as you pay their fares again I'll carry them to anywhere else you wish."

"You're a mercenary bastard, Grimes, aren't you? But *we* shall not be paying their fares. *They* will not be paying their fares. On the contrary, *you'll* be paying them. Wages, at the Award rate."

"*What?*"

"You heard me, Grimes. After all, merchant vessels quite often carry officer cadets."

"Who have had the required pre-Space training at some recognized academy. And I'm sure that there's no such an academy on New Alice."

"There's not. But there are such things as STS— Straight To Space—cadets."

Grimes, who since he had become a merchant spaceman had made a study of all the regulations that could possibly affect him, ransacked his memory.

He said, "But Shirl and Darleen just aren't qualified in any possible way. Aboard a spaceship they'd be completely unskilled personnel."

"But with qualifications, Grimes." He opened

one of the folders on his desk, began to read from it. " 'Any person who has held commissioned rank in the armed forces of any federated planet, wishing to embark upon a new career in the Merchant Service, may serve the qualifying time for the lowest grade of certificate of competency in any merchant vessels, with the rank and pay of officer cadet.' "

"But . . . Commissioned rank?" asked Grimes.

Then he realized that Damien was right. New Sparta was a federated planet. Elena's Amazon Guard had been part of the armed forces of that planet. Shirl and Darleen had held commissions—as officer instructors, but commissions nonetheless—in that body.

"Too," said Damien, grinning again, "both young ladies are now Probationary Ensigns, Special Branch, in the Federation Survey Service Reserve. Of course, their reserve commissions are as secret as yours is. But when I got the first reports, by Carlottigram, from Commander Lazenby about what was happening on New Sparta I decided that I, that we could make use of the special skills and talents of those New Alicians. After all, you did. On Venusberg first of all, then on New Sparta. . . ."

"And your Special Branch," grumbled Grimes, "is one sprouting many strange fruits and flowers."

"Well said. You have the soul of a poet, young Grimes. Anyhow when, in the fullness of time, your *Sister Sue* lifts off you will have, on your Articles, in addition to your normal complement, officer cadets Shirl Kelly and Darleen Byrne . . ."

"Kelly and Byrne?"

"Why not? I explained to the young ladies that they would have to adopt surnames and told them that Kelly and Byrnes are both names associated with Australian history."

"But they were bushrangers, sir."

"Don't be snobbish, Grimes. After all, you've been a pirate yourself."

"A privateer," snapped Grimes. "And acting under your secret orders."

"Which included, at the finish, committing an act of real piracy. But enough of this quibbling. Tomorrow a Mr. Steerforth will be reporting to you as your new chief officer. He will be on loan from the Interstellar Transport Commission. He is also a lieutenant commander in the Survey Service Reserve. He is a capable and experienced officer. Give him a day to settle in and then you'll be free to inflict yourself on your parents in Alice Springs for three weeks. It will be all of that before anybody gets around to discharge your cargo and before your next charter has been arranged."

"Thank you, sir. But can you tell me anything about the next charter? Time, or voyage? Where to?"

"Not yet. Oh, would you mind taking Shirl and Darleen with you to the Alice? They want to see something of inland Australia and you'd make a good guide. I'm sure that your parents wouldn't mind putting up a couple of guests."

His father wouldn't, Grimes thought, but regarding his mother he was far from certain. Even so he was looking forward to seeing Shirl and Darleen again.

Chapter 3

As promised, Mr. Steerforth reported on board shortly after breakfast the following morning. He was tall, blond, deeply tanned, with regular features, startling blue eyes and what seemed to be slightly too many gleaming white teeth. Grimes couldn't be sure, at short acquaintance, whether he liked him or not. He was too much the big ship officer, with too obvious a parade of efficiency. His predecessor, Billy Williams, had been out of the Dog Star Line whose vessels, at their very best, were no more than glorified tramps. (But Williams had always got things done, in his own way, and done well.)

"My gear's on board, sir," said Steerforth briskly. "If it's all right with you I'll nip across to the shipping office and get myself signed on. And then, perhaps, you might introduce me to the other officers, after which you can give me any special instructions. I understand that you are wanting to catch the late afternoon flight to Alice Springs."

"I suppose that the admiral has already given you your instructions," grumbled Grimes.

"The admiral, sir?"

"Come off it, Mr. Steerforth. You know who I mean. Rear Admiral Damien. You're one of his boys."

"If you say so, sir."

"I've said it. All right, go and get your name on the Articles. You should be back in time for morning coffee, when I'll introduce you to the rest of the crowd in the wardroom."

"Very good, sir."

Grimes' next callers were Shirl and Darleen. They knew the ship, of course, having traveled in her, as passengers, from New Sparta to Earth. Certainly they were familiar enough with Grimes' own quarters. . . .

"Hi, John," said Shirl (or was it Darleen?).

"Hi, John," said Darleen (or was it Shirl?).

Had the girls been unclothed Grimes could have told them apart; there were certain minor skin blemishes. But now, dressed as they were in shorts (very short shorts) and shirt outfits they were as alike as two peas in a pod. The odd jointure of their legs was not concealed by their scanty lower garments, their thighs looked powerful (as they were in fact). Wide smiles redeemed the rather long faces under the short brown hair from mere pleasant plainness.

"The Bureau of Colonial Affairs has been looking after us really well," said one of the girls, "but it is good to be back aboard your ship again. The old crocodile has told us that we are to be part of your crew."

The old crocodile? wondered Grimes, then realized that this must be yet another nickname for Admiral Damien.

"He has already made us officers," said Shirl. (Grimes remembered that her voice was very slightly higher than that of Darleen.) "In the Survey Service. But it is supposed to be a secret, although he said that you would know."

"I do," said Grimes.

"And now we are to be officers aboard your ship," Darleen told him unnecessarily.

"And you are to show us the inland of this country of yours, from which our ancestors came. We have seen kangaroos in the zoo in Adelaide, of course, but we have yet to see them in the wild, where they belong. "

"Where *we* belong," said Darleen, a little wistfully. "You know, John, I have often thought that that genetic engineer, all those hundreds of years ago, did the wrong thing when he changed our ancestors. . . ."

"If he hadn't changed them," pointed out Shirl, "*we* shouldn't be here now."

"I suppose not." Darleen's face lit up with a smile. "And it is good being here, with John."

"Mphm," grunted Grimes.

The three of them caught the afternoon flight from Woomera to Alice Springs.

Grimes loved dirigibles, and a flight by airship in charming company was an enjoyable experience. He had a few words with an attentive stewardess, scribbled a few words on the back of one of his business cards for her to take to the captain and, shortly thereafter, he and the two New Alicians were ushered into the control cab. The girls stared out through the wide windows at the sunburned landscape flowing astern beneath them, with the greenery around irrigation lakes and ditches in vivid contrast to the dark browns of the more normal landscape, peered through borrowed binoculars at the occasional racing emu, exclaimed with delight as they spotted a mob of kangaroos. But the shadows cast by rocks and hillocks were lengthening as the sun sagged down to the horizon. Soon there would be nothing to see but the scattered lights of villages and townships.

"This must seem a very slow means of transport to you, Captain," said the airship's master.

"After all, when you're used to exceeding the speed of light . . ."

"But not with scenery like this to look at, Captain," said Grimes.

"The two young ladies seem to be appreciating it," said the airshipman. "They're not Terran, are they?"

"No, although their ancestors were both Terran and Australian. They're from a world called New Alice."

"The name rings no bell. Would it be one of the lost colonies?"

"Yes."

"I saw a piece on trivi about Morrowvia a few months ago. . . . The world of the cat people. . . . If I ever save enough for an off-planet holiday I might go there. Say, wasn't it you who discovered, or rediscovered, that Lost Colony?"

"Not exactly. But I was there during the period when it was decided that the Morrowvians were legally human."

The airship captain lowered his voice. "And these young ladies with you. . . . From New Alice, you say. Would they be the end result of some nutty experiment by some round the bend genetic engineer?"

Shirl and Darleen possessed abnormal, by human standards, hearing. They turned as one away from the window to face the airshipman. They smiled sweetly.

"Yes, captain," said Shirl. "Although we are legally human our ancestors were not, as yours are, monkeys."

If the captain was embarrassed he did not show it. He looked them up and down in a manner that suggested that he was mentally undressing them. He grinned at them cheerfully.

"Tie me kangaroo down, sport," he chuckled. "I shouldn't mind gettin' the chance to tie you down!"

"You could try," said Darleen slowly.

"And it could be the last thing you ever did try," said Shirl.

They were still smiling, the pair of them, but Grimes knew that it was more of a vicious baring of teeth than anything else.

The airshipman broke the tense silence.

"Excuse me, ladies. Excuse me, Captain. I'd better start thinkin' about gettin' the old girl to her mooring mast at the Alice." He addressed his first officer. "Mr. Cleary, confirm our ETA with airport control, will you? Ask 'em about conditions—surface wind and all the rest of it. . . ."

Why tell me to do what I always do? said Cleary's expression as plainly as spoken words.

"Shall we get out of your way, now, Captain?" asked Grimes.

"Oh, no, Captain. Just keep well aft in the cab." He managed a laugh. "Who knows? You might learn something."

But it wasn't the airshipman's day. He bumbled his first approach to mast, slid past it with only millimeters of clearance. He had to bring his ship around to make a second try. He blamed a sudden shift of wind for the initial bungle but he knew—and Grimes knew—that it was nothing of the kind. It was no more and no less than the result of an attempt to impress a hostile female audience.

Chapter 4

Grimes' parents were waiting in the lounge at the base of the mooring mast. His mother embraced him, his father took his hand and grasped it warmly between both of his. Then Grimes introduced the two girls. He realized that he could not remember which one had been given Kelly as a surname and which one was Byrne. Why the hell, he asked himself, couldn't Damien have had them entered in the books as sisters? As twin sisters, even. They looked enough alike. (Some little time later he raised this point with the two New Alicians. "But the admiral is very thorough, John," Darleen told him. "To put us down as being related would have made nonsense of his files. It was explained to us. It is all a matter of blood groups and such. . . .")

The older people did, as a matter of fact, look rather puzzled when Shirl and Darleen were introduced. But they asked no questions and, in any case, the Grimes household was one in which the use of given names was the rule rather than the exception.

Baggage was collected and then the party boarded the family hovercar. Grimes senior took the road in a direction away from the city, deviated from this on to what was little more than a rough track, heading toward what the old man called his private oasis. By now it was quite dark and overhead the black sky was ablaze with stars. In the spreading beam of the headlights green eyes gleamed with reflected radiance from the low brush on either side of the track. For a while an old man kangaroo bounded ahead of the vehicle until, at last, it collected its wits and broke away to the right, out of the path of the car.

The lights came on in the house as the hovercar approached. His father was still doing well, thought the spaceman, could still afford all the latest in robotic home help. The wide drive, dull-gleaming permaplast bordered with ornamental shrubs, had been swept clear of the dust that here, in the Red Center, got everywhere. Ahead, the wide door of the big garage slid up and open. The old man reduced speed at the very last moment and slid smoothly into the brilliantly lit interior. Gently sighing, the vehicle subsided in its skirts.

Grimes senior was first out of the car. Gallantly he assisted the ladies to alight—not that any of them needed his aid—leaving his son to cope with the baggage. A door slid open in one of the side walls. In it stood a woman—a *transparent* woman? No, not a woman. A robot in human female form, with what appeared to be delicate, beautifully fashioned, gleaming clockwork innards, some of the fragile-seeming wheels spinning rapidly, others with a barely perceptible movement.

"Come in," said this obviously hellishly expensive automaton. "This is Liberty Hall. You can spit on the mat and call the cat a bastard."

"Cor stiffen the bleeding crows!" said Grimes.

Matilda Grimes laughed without much humour. "Just one of George's latest toys," she said. "It came programmed with a standard vocabulary but he added to it."

"Too right," said the robot in a pleasant contralto.

"I like her," maintained George Whitley Grimes.

"You would," his wife told him.

Meanwhile it—she?—advanced on Grimes, arms extended. What was he supposed to do? he wondered. Shake hands? Throw his own arms about the thing in a step-brotherly embrace?

"Let her have the bags, John," said his father.

It took them from him, managing them with contemptuous ease, led the way into the house. The workings of the machinery in her hips and

legs was fascinatingly obvious. It was like, in a
way, one of those beautiful antique clocks that
spend their working lives in glass domes. And
what would it be like, he wondered, to make love
to an eight day clock? *Down, boy, down!* he snarled
mentally at his, at times kinky, libido.

They sat in the big, comfortable lounge, Shirl and
Darleen in very deep armchairs that caused them
to make a display of their long, long legs. Grimes
noticed that his father's eyes kept straying toward
the two New Alicians. Perhaps, he thought, it
was no more than biological curiosity. Those am-
ply displayed lower limbs were not quite human.
Or perhaps the old man was betraying another
sort of biological interest. Grimes could not blame
him. Like son, like father. . . .

"Shirl," asked Matilda Grimes sweetly. "Darleen
. . . Aren't you chilly? Wouldn't you like to put
on something warmer?"

"It is quite all right, Matilda," said Shirl. "We
often wear less than this. John can tell you. . . ."

His mother looked at him coldly and said, "You
never change much, do you? I remember when
you were only twelve, when we were living in
that old house in Flynn Street, and you appointed
yourself secretary of the Flynn Street Nudist Club
which held its meetings by the pool in our back-
yard . . . As I recall it, you were the only male
member."

"And I had to shift my workroom to the front of the house," said George Whitley Grimes. "The view from the back windows was too distracting."

"And I," said Matilda, "had to cope with an irate committee of local mothers who had discovered how their little bitches of daughters were spending their afternoons . . ."

"And I," said George, "had to stay away from the pub for fear of being beaten up by the fathers of those same little bitches."

Shirl and Darleen laughed.

"You Earthpeople, as we are discovering, have such odd ways of looking at things," said one of them.

"Not all of us," said Grimes senior. "And not any of us for all of the time."

The robutler rolled in with the pre-dinner drinks. It was an even bigger and more elaborate model than the one that had been in service at the time of Grimes's last visit to the parental home, reminding him of a suit of mechanized battle armor built to accommodate at least three Federation Marines simultaneously. With it came the house robot that Grimes was now thinking of as Clockwork Kitty. Like its predecessor the robutler took spoken orders and, in its capacious interior, seemed to hold a stock of every alcoholic drink known to civilized Man—and, quite possibly, a few that weren't. There were ice cubes, spa water and fruit cordials. There was a fine selection of little eats.

As the various orders were extruded on trays they were deftly removed by Clockwork Kitty and handed to the correct recipients. Bowls of nuts and dishes of tiny savories were placed on convenient low tables.

George Whitley Grimes raised his condensation-misted glass of beer to his son and said, "Here's to crime!"

The two girls, who also were drinking beer, raised their glasses. Grimes raised his glass of pink gin. Matilda Grimes set her sherry down firmly on the table.

"That," she stated, "is a dangerous toast to be drinking in the presence of this son of mine. I still have not forgotten that court of inquiry into the piracy with which he was involved. We have yet to hear, from his lips, the full story of what happened when he was Governor of Liberia—but I have little doubt that there were more than a few illegalities. . . ."

"Not committed by me, Matilda," Grimes told her. "Don't forget that I was the Law, trying to put a stop to other people's illegal profits."

"Hah!" his mother snorted. "Oh, well, you weren't impeached. I suppose that we must thank the Odd Gods of the Galaxy for small mercies. But we have yet to hear about what really happened on New Sparta. . . ."

"You shall, my dear, you shall." He laughed. "Oh, I was guilty of one crime. I did 'borrow' a Survey Service courier. . . ."

"And you crashed it," said Darleen a little maliciously.

"It was the fault of the weather," said Grimes.

Matilda laughed. "All right, all right. And I suppose that you still hold that reserve commission in the Survey Service that's supposed to be such a secret and get sent hither and yon to do that man Damien's dirty work for him." She looked long and hard at Shirl and Darleen. "And am I right in assuming that the pair of you are also members of the good admiral's department of dirty tricks?"

The girls looked inquiringly at Grimes. He decided that he had better answer for them.

"If you must know—but keep it strictly to yourself—Shirl and Darleen are both probationary ensigns in the Service."

"And what is their specialty?" asked Matilda.

"Unarmed combat," Grimes told her. "Or combat with anything handy, and preferably sharp, that can be flung. Such as . . ."

Shirl picked up a shallow, round dish that was now empty. She turned it over so that its convexity was on the down side. With a sharp flick of her wrist she threw it from her. It circled the room, returned to her waiting hand.

"Flying saucers yet!" said Grimes's father.

*   *   *

After a second drink they went in to the dinner
that was served by the efficient Clockwork Kitty.
With the first course there was some slight embarrassment. It was Grimes's fault, of course. (But
just about everything was.) He should have told
his mother that the ancestors of the New Alicians
had been kangaroos. Even though these people
were now classed as human and, like true humans descended from the original killer ape,
omnivorous, they refused kangaroo tail soup, once
they learned what it was. But they had strong
stomachs and enjoyed the excellent crown roast
of lamb once they had been assured that it was of
ovine origin.

Grimes himself managed a good dinner despite
the fact that he was talking most of the time. He
had not been able to visit his parents on the first
occasion of his return to Earth from Liberia, via
New Sparta. A very thorough debriefing had occupied practically all of his time. So now there
were questions to be answered, stories to be told.
He was still answering questions and telling stories when the party returned to the lounge for
coffee and brandy. Grimes and his father smoked
their pipes, Matilda cigarillo and Shirl and Darleen—they were picking up bad habits—cigarettes
in long, elegant, bejeweled holders.

Finally Darleen seemed to be having trouble

stifling a yawn. It was infectious. George said, "I don't know about you people, but I'm turning in." Darleen said, "If you do not mind, Matilda, we shall do so too."

Matilda grinned. "Not with my old man, you won't! The maid will show you to your rooms."

Clockwork Kitty led them away, leaving Grimes alone with his mother.

She smiled at him a little sadly. She said, "I need hardly ask you, John, need I? But, just to satisfy my curiosity, which one is it?"

Grimes was frank.

"Both of them," he said.

"What! Not both at once?"

As a matter of fact this had been known but Grimes' mother was, in some ways, rather prudish. And, apart from anything else, there was the matter of miscegenation. The old prejudice against the underpeople still lingered.

"Shirl," lied Grimes.

"I really don't know how you can tell one from the other. Well, John, you're a big boy now, a four ring captain and a shipowner, and you've been a planetary governor . . . And commodore of a pirate squadron," she added maliciously. "You're old enough and wicked enough to look after yourself. And the girls' rooms are next to yours in the west wing.

"But I do wish that you would find some nice, *human* girl and settle down. Isn't it time?"

"I'll get around to it eventually," he promised
her.

He kissed her good night then made his way to
his quarters. The double bed, he saw, was already
occupied. By Shirl.

And Darleen.

Chapter 5

"Wakey, wakey!" caroled an annoyingly cheerful female voice. There was a subdued clatter as the tea tray was placed on the bedside table. Morning sunlight flooded the room as curtains were drawn back. "Rise and shine! Rise and shine for the Black Ball Line!"

Grimes unglued his eyelids and looked up at Clockwork Kitty as she stood over the tousled bed, the rays of the sun glitteringly reflected from the intricacy of moving clockwork under her transparent integument. (But those delicate wheels, on their jeweled pivots, were no more than decoration, an expensive camouflage for the real machinery of metal skeleton and powerful solenoids.) Somehow her vaguely oriental features, which pos-

sessed a limited mobility, managed to register
disapproval. Although Shirl and Darleen had returned to their own rooms before dawn, it was
obvious, from the state of the bed, that Grimes
had not slept alone.

He blinked. Yes, that faint sneer was still there.
A trick of the light? Just how intelligent was this
robomaid? Oh, he was thinking of Clockwork Kitty
as *she*—but spacemen are apt to think of almost
any piece of mobile machinery as *she*. Just another example of his father's sense of humor, he
decided. The old man had added certain expres-
sions to her programming, just as he had added to
her vocabulary. An historical novelist with a keen
interest in maritime history would, of course, know
the words of quite a few of the old sea chanteys,
such as "rise and shine for the Black Ball Line" . . .

"Milk, sir? Sugar?"

The automaton poured and stirred efficiently,
putting the milk and sugar into the cup first.
(And that, remembered Grimes, was something
that his mother always insisted on.)

"Thank you, Kitty," he said. (It cost nothing to
be polite to robots, intelligent or not. And when
one wasn't quite sure of a robot's actual intelligence it was better to play it safe.)

"Kitty, sir?"

"My name for you. When I first saw you I
thought of you as 'Clockwork Kitty.' "

"The master's name for me," said the robomaid,

"is Seiko. I was manufactured by the Seiko Corporation in Japan, the makers of this planet's finest household robots. Prior to our highly successful venture into the field of robotics we were, and indeed still are, the makers of this planet's finest timepieces. Robomaids such as myself are a memorial, as it were, to the Corporation's origins ..."

"Yes, yes," Grimes interrupted hastily. What was coming out now was some of the original programming, a high-powered advertising spiel. "Very interesting, Kitty—sorry, Seiko. But I'd rather be getting showered, depilated and all the rest of it. What time is breakfast?"

"If you will make your order, sir, it will be ready shortly after you appear in the breakfast room."

"Surprise me," said Grimes.

He looked thoughtfully after the glittering figure as it moved silently and gracefully out of the room.

Grimes senior, who was a breakfast table conservative, tucked in to a large plate of fried eggs, bacon, sausages and country fried potatoes. Matilda toyed with a croissant and strawberry conserve. Shirl and Darleen seemed to be enjoying helpings of kedgeree. And for Grimes, after he had finished his half grapefruit, Seiko produced one of his favorite dishes, and one that he had

not enjoyed for quite a long time. The plump
kippers, served with a side plate of thickly cut
new brown bread and butter, tasted as good as
they looked.

Matilda, he decided, must have told Seiko what
he would like. He commented on this. She, looking surprised, said that she had given no orders
whatsoever regarding her son's meal.

So ... A lucky guess? Do robots guess? But
Seiko was absent in the kitchen so he could not
make further inquiries until she returned to clear
the table. And when she did so the humans were
busy discussing the day's activities.

George Grimes said, "I'm afraid that I shall
have to leave you young people to your own
resources today. I've a deadline to meet. The trouble with the novel I'm working on now is that I'm
having to work on it. It's just not writing itself."

"Why not, George?" asked Grimes.

"Because it's set in a period of Australian history that, somehow, makes no great appeal to me.
Eureka Stockade and all that. I somehow can't
empathize with any of the characters. And, although it's regarded by rather too many histori-
ans as a minor revolution that might have blown
up into something larger, it was nothing of the
kind. It was no more than a squalid squabble
between tax evaders and tax collectors. But I got a
handsome advance before I started writing it, so
I'd better deliver on time."

"And I have to stay in today myself," said Matilda. "I've got the ladies of the Alice Springs Literary Society coming round for lunch. I'm afraid that you'd find them as boring as all hell—as I do myself, frankly. So why not take the car, John, and a packed midday meal, and just cruise around? I'd suggest Ayers Rock and the Olgas, but at this time of the year they're *infested* with tourists. But the desert itself is always fascinating."

And so it was that, an hour later, Grimes, Shirl and Darleen were speeding away from the low, rambling house, heading out over the almost featureless desert, the great plume of fine, red dust raised by the vehicle's fans swirling in their wake.

Grimes gave Ayers Rock and Mount Olga a wide berth—the one squatting on the horizon like a huge, red toad, the other looking like some domed city erected on an airless planet. Over each hovered a sizeable fleet of tourist dirigibles. Grimes could imagine what conditions would be like on the ground—the souvenir stalls, the refreshment stands, the canned music, the milling crowds. Some time he would have to visit the Rock and the Olgas again, but not today.

He came to the Uluru Irrigation Canal. He did not cross it but followed its course south. The artificial waterway was poorly maintained; the agricultural project that it had been designed to service had been cancelled, largely due to pres-

sure by the conservationists. But water still flowed
sluggishly in the ditch and, here and there along
its length, were billabongs, one of which Grimes
had known very well in his youth. It would be
good, he hoped, to visit it again.

And there were the tall ghost gums standing
around and among the water-worn rocks that some
civil engineer with the soul of a landscape gar-
dener had brought in, probably at great expense,
to make the artificial pool look natural. And there
was the water, inviting, surprisingly clear, its surface dotted here and there with floating blossoms.
These were not of Terran origin but were, as a
matter of fact, Grimes' own contribution to the
amenities of this pleasant oasis, carnivorous plants,
insectivores, from Caribbea. The billabong was
free from mosquitoes and other such pests. (He
recalled that some businessman had wanted to
import these flowers in quantity but the conservationists had screamed about upsetting the balance
of nature.)

He stopped the car just short of the ornamental
bounders. He and the girls got out, walked to the
steeply shelving beach of red sand. He said, "How
about a swim?"

"Crocodiles?" asked Shirl dubiously.

"There weren't any last time I was here."

"When was that?" asked Darleen.

"Oh, about five Earth years ago."

He got out of his shirt, shorts and underthings,

kicked off his sandals. As one the girls peeled the white T shirts from the upper parts of their tanned bodies, stepped out of their netherwear. Naked, long-legged and small-breasted, they seemed to belong to this landscape, more than did Grimes himself. They waded out into the deeper water. Grimes followed them. The temperature of the sun-warmed pool was pleasant. They played like overgrown children with a beach ball that some family party had left on the sand. (So other people had found his private billabong, thought Grimes. He hoped that they had enjoyed it as much as he was doing now.) They decorated each other's bodies with the gaudy water lilies, the tendrils of which clung harmlessly to their wet skins. Finally they emerged from the water and stretched themselves to dry off on the surface of a large, flat rock which was partially shielded from the harsh sunlight by the ghost gums.

Then Grimes felt hungry. He got to his feet and walked to the hover car, taking from it the hamper that had been packed by Seiko. The sandwiches were to his taste—ham with plenty of mustard, a variety of strong cheeses—and the girls enjoyed the sweet and savory pastries and the fresh fruits. The cans of beer, from their own special container, were nicely chilled.

Replete, Grimes got his pipe and tobacco from his clothing and indulged in a satisfying smoke.

The New Alicians sat on either side of him in oddly prim postures, their legs tucked under them.

Grimes was feeling poetic.

" 'Give me a book of verses 'neath the bough,' " he quoted,

" 'A loaf of bread, a flask of wine, and thou,

" 'Beside me, singing in the wilderness . . .

" 'And wilderness were Paradise enow.' "

He laughed. "But I don't have a book of verses. And, come to that, I've never heard either of you singing. . . ."

"There is a time to sing. . . ." murmured Shirl. "And this could be such a time. . . ."

And Darleen had found two large, smooth pebbles, about the size of golf balls, and was clicking them together with an odd, compelling rhythm. Both girls were crooning softly to the beat of the singing stones. There was melody, of a sort, soft and hypnotic. Grimes felt the goose pimples rising all over his skin.

They were not alone. He and the girls were not alone. Silently the kangaroos had come from what had seemed to be empty desert, were standing all around them, regarding them solemnly with their huge eyes. There were big reds and grays and smaller animals. It was as though every variety of kangaroo in all of Australia had answered the New Alicians' summons.

Shirl and Darleen got to their feet. And then, suddenly, they were gone, bounding away over the desert at the head of the mob of kangaroos. It was hard to distinguish them from the animals despite their smooth skins.

What now? wondered Grimes. *What now?* He was, he supposed, responsible for the girls. Should he get into the hover car and give chase? Or would that make matters worse? He stood and watched the cloud of red dust, raised by the myriad bounding feet, diminishing in the distance.

But they were coming back, just the two of them, just Shirl and Darleen. They were running gracefully, not proceeding in a series of bounds. They flung themselves on Grimes, their sweaty, dusty bodies hot against his bare skin. It was rape, although the man was a willing enough victim. They had him, both of them, in turn, again and again.

Finally, exhausted, they rolled off him.

"After the kangaroos . . ." gasped Shirl.

"We had to prove to ourselves . . ." continued Darleen.

". . . and to you . . ."

". . . that we are really human . . ."

Grimes found his pipe, which, miraculously, had not been broken during the assault, and his pouch, the contents of which were unspilled. He lit up with a not very steady hand.

"Of course you're human," he said at last. "The Law says so."

"But the heritage is strong, John."

"You aren't the only ones with a heritage—but you don't see me swinging from the branches of trees, do you?"

They all laughed then, and shared the last can of beer, and had a last refreshing swim in the waters of the billabong. They resumed their clothing and got back into the hover car, looking forward to an enjoyable evening of good food and conversation to add the finishing touches to what had been a very enjoyable day.

They were not expecting to find the Grimes home knee deep in acrimony.

Chapter 6

The garage door slid open as the hovercar approached but the robomaid was not waiting to receive them and to take custody of the empty hamper. Grimes was not concerned about this; no doubt, he thought, Seiko was busy with some domestic task. He led the two girls into the house, toward the lounge. He heard the voices of his mother and father, although it was his mother who seemed to be doing most of the talking. She sounded as though she were in what her husband and son referred to as one of her flaring rages. *What's the old man been up to now?* wondered Grimes.

"Either that *thing* goes or I go!" he heard his mother declare.

"But I find her more satisfactory . . ." his father said.

"You would. You've a warped mind, George Grimes, as I've known, to my cost, for years. But you'll ship that toy of yours back to Tokyo and demand your money back. . . ."

"Hi, folks," said Grimes as he entered the room.

Matilda favored him with no more than a glance, his father looked toward him appealingly.

"John," he said, "perhaps you can talk some sense into your mother. You, as a space captain of long experience, know far more about such matters than either of us. . . ."

"What matters?" asked Grimes.

"You may well ask," Matilda told him. "Such matters as insubordination, mutiny. In my own home. . . ."

"Insubordination? Mutiny?" repeated Grimes in a puzzled voice.

"And unprovoked assault upon my guests. *My* guests."

Grimes sat down, pulled his pipe from his pocket, filled and lit it. Shirl and Darleen did not take seats but looked questioningly at Matilda, who said, "Perhaps, dears, it might be better if you went to your rooms for a while. This is a family matter."

The girls left, albeit with reluctance. Grimes settled down in his chair and assumed a magisterial pose. George Grimes was sitting on the edge of his seat, looking as uncomfortable as he almost certainly was feeling.

"I have had my suspicions for a long time . . ." began Matilda.

Surely not . . . wondered Grimes. The old man's not that kinky . . .

"Quite a long time," she went on. "But it was only after you and the girls had left this morning for your ride in the desert that I began to be sure. I hope that you had a pleasant day, by the way. . . ."

"Very pleasant," said Grimes.

"Well, you remember what you had for breakfast. Kippers. You asked me if I'd told it to do them for you. I said that I had not. I was curious, so I asked it why it had served you kippers. It told me that you had asked it to surprise you. So I asked it how it had decided that kippers would be a nice surprise. It told me that normally there are never kippers in my larder but that I had ordered a supply after I'd gotten word that you were coming. . . ."

"And so?" asked Grimes.

"A domestic robot is supposed to do only what it's been programmed to do. It's not supposed to possess such qualities as initiative and imagination. Oh, I know that there are some truly intelligent robots—but such are very, very expensive and are not to be found doing menial jobs. But knowing

George, I suspected that he had been doing some
more tinkering with *its* programming. His idea of
a joke.

"Well, as you already know, I was entertaining
the local literary ladies to luncheon. The Presi-
lent of the Society is Dame Mabel Prendergast.
Don't ask me how she got made a dame, although
she's made an enormous pile of money writing
slush. She could afford to buy a title. Anyhow,
dear Mabel is just back from a galactic cruise. She
was all tarted up in obviously expensive clothing
in the very worst of taste that she had purchased
on the various worlds that she had visited. Her
hat, she told us, came from Carinthia, where glass-
weaving is one of the esteemed arts and crafts.
Oh, my dear, it was a most elaborate construction,
perched on top of her head like a sort of glittering
fairy castle. It was, in its way, beautiful—but not
on her. Human hippopotami should not wear such
things.

"We had lunch. *It* did the serving, just as a
robomaid should, efficiently and without any
gratuitous displays of initiative, imagination or
whatever. The ladies admired *it* and Mabel remarked, rather jealously, that George's thud-and-
blunder books, as she referred to them, must be
doing quite well. We retired to the lounge for
coffee and brandy and then one or two of the old
biddies started making inquiries about my famous
son. *You.* And wasn't it time that you settled

down? And who were the two pretty girls you'd brought with you? They weren't Terran, were they?

"I told them—all the more fool me, but I suppose that the brandy had loosened my tongue—that Shirl and Darleen were from a world called New Alice, with a very Australianoid culture. I told them, too, that they were now junior officers aboard your ship and that, until recently, they had been officers in the elite Amazon Guard on New Sparta. Mabel said that they didn't look butch military types. I said that, as a matter of fact, they had been officer instructors, specializing in teaching the use of throwing weapons, such as boomerangs. And that they could make almost anything behave like a boomerang. Mabel said that she didn't think that this was possible. I told her that Shirl—or was it Darleen?—had given a demonstration in this very room, using a round, shallow dish . . .

"Mabel said, quite flatly, that this would be quite impossible and started blathering about the laws of aerodynamics. She had, she assured us, made a thorough study of these before writing her latest book, about a handsome young professional hang glider racer and a lady trapeze artiste. . . ."

"Did they . . . er . . . mate in midair?" asked Grimes interestedly.

"Your mind is as low as your father's," Matilda told him crossly. "Anyhow, there was this argument. And *it*—may its clockwork heart rust solid!

—decided, very kindly, to settle it for us. It asked, very politely, "May I demonstrate, madam?" and before I could say no it emptied the chocolate mints out of their dish, on to the table, turned the dish upside down and with a flick of its wrist sent it sailing around the room . . .

"Oh, it did actually come back—but just out of reach of that uppity robot's outstretched hand. It crashed into Dame Mabel's hat. That hat, it seems, was so constructed as to be proof against all normal stresses and strains but there must have been all sorts of tensions locked up in its strands. When the dish—it was one of those copper ones—hit it there was an explosion, with glass splinters and powder flying in all directions. By some miracle nobody was seriously hurt, although old Tanitha Evans got a rather bad cut and Lola Lee got powdered glass in her right eye. I had to send for Dr. Namatjira—and you know what *he* charges for house calls. And, of course, I shall have to pay for Dame Mabel's hat. Anybody would think that the bloody thing was made of diamonds!"

"And where is Seiko now?" asked Grimes.

"Seiko? *It*, you mean. It is back in the crate that it came in, and there it stays. It's too dangerous to be allowed to run around loose."

"She was only trying to be helpful," said Grimes.

"It's not its job to try to be helpful. It's its job to do as it's told, just that and nothing more."

"What do you know about the so-called wild robots, John?" asked his father suddenly.

"Not much. The roboticists are rather close-mouthed about such matters. Even the Survey Service does not have access to all the information it should. Oh, there are standing orders to deal with such cases. They boil down to Deactivate At Once And Return To Maker or, if deactivation is not practicable, Destroy By Any Means Possible."

"Just what I've been telling George," said Matilda smugly.

"But from your experience, which is much greater than mine, how would you define a wild robot?" asked George.

"Mphm," grunted Grimes. "Well, there are robots, not necessarily humanoid, which are designed to be intelligent and which acquire very real characters. There was Big Sister, the computer-pilot of the Baroness Michelle d'Estang's space-yacht. There was a Mr. Adam, with whom I tangled, many, many years ago when I was a Survey Service courier captain. There have been others. All of them were designed to be rational, thinking beings. But a normal pilot-computer is no more than an automatic pilot. It does no more than what it's been programmed to. If some emergency crops up that has not been included in its programming it just sits on its metaphorical backside and does nothing."

"But the rogue robots," persisted George. "The wild robots. . . ."

"I don't know. But among spacemen there are all sorts of theories. One is that there has been some slight error made during the manufacture of the . . . the brain. May as well call it that. Some undetectable defect in a microchip. A defect that really isn't a defect at all, since it achieves a result that would be hellishly expensive if done on purpose. Another theory is that exposure to radiation is the cause. And there's one really far-fetched one—association with humans of more than average intelligence and creativity."

"I like that," said George.

"You would, Herr Doktor Frankenstein," sneered Matilda. "But, from what I've told you, do you think that we've a wild robot on our hands, John?"

"It seems like it," said Grimes.

The next morning the carriers came to remove the crate into which Seiko had been packed. Grimes went with his father into the storeroom, watched with some regret as the spidery stowbot picked up the long, coffin-like box and carried it out to the waiting hovervan. He thought nothing of it when George ran out to the vehicle before it departed, to exchange a few words with the driver and, it seemed, to resecure the label on the crate, which must have come loose.

George rejoined his son.

THE WILD ONES 55

"Well," he said, "that's that. Luckily Matilda's a good cook; like you, she can get the best out of an autochef. You and the girls won't starve for the remainder of your stay here."

Nor did they.

Chapter 7

The days passed quickly. George Whitley Grimes had gotten over his sulks about being deprived of his glittering toy and Matilda Grimes had forgiven her husband for the damage done by Seiko. The two girls fitted into the family life well. "They're much too nice for you, John," his mother told him one morning over coffee. The two of them had gone into Alice Springs on a shopping expedition and were enjoying refreshment in one of the better cafés. (George was still working on his Eureka Stockade novel and Shirl and Darleen had gone off to practice with the traditional boomerangs that they had been given by Dr. Namatjira, whose calls now were social rather than professional.)

"They're much too nice, for you," she said. "And I'm not at all sure that I approve of their traveling in your ship as crew members, among all those brutal and licentious spacemen."

"And spacewomen." He laughed. "My third officer is Tomoko Suzuki, a real Japanese doll. . . ."

"Not like Seiko, I hope."

"No. Her innards aren't on display. And my radio officer is Cleo Jones, black and beautiful. Her nickname, of which she's rather proud, is the Zulu Princess. The second Mannschenn Drive engineer is Sarah Smith. One of those tall, slim, handsome academic females. Three of the inertial/ reaction drive engineers, the chief, second and fourth, are women. The chief's name is Florence Scott. She looks like what she is, an extremely competent mechanic, and her sex somehow doesn't register. The second is Juanita Garcia. If you were casting an amateur production of *Carmen* you'd try to get her for the title role. She has the voice as well as the looks. The fourth is Cassandra Perkins. Like Cleo, she's a negress. But she's short and plump and very jolly, so much so that she gets away with things that anybody else would be hauled over the coals for. . . ."

"Such as . . . ?"

"Such as the time when she was doing some minor repairs to the ship's plumbing system and bungled some fantastic cross-connection so that the hot water taps ran ice water."

"That might have been intentional. Her idea of a joke."

"If it was, the laugh was on her. She was the first victim. She thought that she'd like a nice, hot shower after she came off watch at midnight, ship's time. Her screams woke all hands." Grimes sipped his coffee and then went on philosophically. "With all her faults, she's a good shipmate. She's fun. Even old Flo, her chief, admits it. What none of us can tolerate is somebody who's highly inefficient *and* a bad shipmate."

"And the other way around?" Matilda asked. "Somebody who's highly efficient but a bad shipmate?"

Grimes sighed. "One just has to suffer such people. My new chief officer seems to be one such. Lieutenant Commander Harald Steerforth, Survey Service Reserve. Harald, with an 'a.' Steerforth. The last of the vikings. Give him a blond beard to match his hair and a horned helmet and he'd look the part. And he's indicated that, as my second in command, he intends to run a taut ship . . ."

"My nose fair bleeds for you," said Matilda inelegantly. "But you haven't mentioned your catering officer yet. Aren't spaceship catering officers almost invariably women?"

"They are. But when I left Port Woomera I still hadn't got a replacement for Magda, who's on leave."

"You should have asked your father for Seiko, and signed *it*—I refuse to call that thing *her*—on."

Shopping done—mainly pieces of Aboriginal artwork as gifts for Shirl and Darleen—Grimes and his mother returned home. When George heard them enter the house he came out from his study and said, "There was a call for you, John. From your ship. Your chief officer, a Mr. Steerforth. He seemed rather annoyed to learn that you hadn't been sitting hunched over the phone all day and every day waiting for him to get in touch." He gave his son a slip of paper. "He asked me—no, damn it, he practically ordered me—to ask you to call him at this number."

The number Grimes recognized. It was the one that had been allocated to his ship at Port Woomera.

"And I shall be greatly obliged," said the old man, "if you will reverse charges."

"Don't be a tightwad, George!" admonished Matilda.

"I'm not a tightwad. This is obviously ship's business. John is a wealthy shipowner; I'm only a poor, struggling writer. And after I've paid for Dame Mabel's hat I shall be even poorer!"

"It was your absurdly expensive mechanical toy that destroyed the hat!"

Grimes left them to it, went to the extention

telephone in his bedroom. He got through without trouble, telling the roboperator to charge the call to his business credit card account. The screen came alive and the pretty face of Tomoko Suzuki appeared. She smiled as she saw Grimes in the screen at her end and said brightly, "Ah, Captain-san. . . ."

"Yes, it's me, Tomoko-san. Can you get Mr. Steerforth for me, please?"

"One moment, Captain-san."

In a remarkably short space of time Tomoko's face in the screen was replaced by that of the chief officer.

"Sir!" said that gentleman smartly.

"Yes, Mr. Steerforth?" asked Grimes.

"Discharge has commenced, sir. I have been informed by Admiral Damien that the Survey Service wishes to charter the ship for a one way voyage to Pleth, with a cargo of stores and equipment for the sub-base on that planet. He wishes to discuss with you details of further employment and intimated that your return to Woomera as soon as possible will be appreciated. . . ."

Not only appreciated by Damien, thought Grimes, but necessary. He had his living to earn.

He said, "I shall return by the first flight tomorrow. Meanwhile, how are things aboard the ship?"

"We have a new catering officer, sir. A Ms. Melinda Clay. She appears to be quite competent.

There is some mail for you, of course. I have opened the business letters and, in accordance with your instructions, dealt with such matters, small accounts and such, as came within my provenance as second in command. Personal correspondence has been untouched."

"Thank you, Mr. Steerforth. I shall see you early tomorrow afternoon."

He hung up, rejoined his parents in the lounge.

"My holiday's over," he announced regretfully. "It was far too short."

"It certainly has been," said Matilda.

"And where are you off to this time, John?" asked his father.

"Pleth. A one voyage charter. Survey Service stores. Probably a full load of forms to be filled out in quintuplicate."

"And after that? Back to Earth with a full load of similar forms filled in?"

"I don't know, George. The mate told me that Damien has some further employment in mind for me."

"No more privateering?" asked the old man a little wistfully. "No more appointments as governor general?"

"I hope not," Grimes told him. "But, knowing Damien, and knowing something of the huge number of pies that he has a finger in, I suspect that it will be something . . . interesting."

"And disreputable, no doubt," snapped Matilda. "When you were a regular officer in the Service you never used to get into all these scrapes."

"Mphm?" grunted Grimes dubiously. He'd been getting into scrapes for as long as he could remember.

Shirl and Alice came in, accompanied by Dr. Namatjira. The doctor, who had joined them at their boomerang practice, was glowing with admiration. "If only I had a time machine!" he exclaimed. "If only I could send them back to the early days of my people in this country, before the white man came! They could have instructed us in the martial arts, especially those involved with the use of flung missiles." He grinned whitely. "Captain Cook, and all those who followed him, would have been driven back into the sea!"

"I might just use that," murmured Grimes senior. "It sounds much more fun that what I'm doing now. That boring Peter Lalor and his bunch of drunken roughnecks. . . ."

Matilda served afternoon tea. After this the doctor said his farewells and made his departure. He expressed the sincere hope that he would be meeting Shirl and Darleen again in the not too distant future.

"Bring them back, John," he admonished. "They belong here. They are like beings from our Dream Time, spirits made flesh . . ."

And then there was what would be the last family dinner for quite some time, with talk lasting long into the night. It would have lasted much longer but Grimes and the girls had an early morning flight to catch.

Chapter 8

It was a pleasant enough flight back to Port Woomera. Again Grimes, and with him the two girls, was a guest in the airship's control cab. On this occasion, however, the captain, a different one, did not say anything to antagonize his privileged passengers. The three of them made their way from the airport to the spaceport by monorail and then by robocab to the ship.

The efficient Mr. Steerforth was waiting by the ramp as the cab pulled up, saluted with Survey Service big ship smartness as his captain got out. He said, "Leave your baggage, sir, I'll have it brought up." He followed Grimes into the after airlock, but not before he had ordered sharply, "Ms. Kelly, Ms. Byrne, look after the master's gear, will you?"

Grimes heard a not quite suppressed animal growl from either Shirl or Darleen and with an effort managed not to laugh aloud. Well, he thought, the two New Alicians would have to start learning that, as cadets, they were the lowest form of life aboard *Sister Sue*. . . .

He and the chief officer took the elevator up to the captain's flat. He let himself into his day cabin, thinking that, much as he had enjoyed the break, it was good to be back. But had somebody been interfering with the layout of the furniture? Had something been added?

Something had—a long case, standing on end.

Steerforth saw him looking at it and said, "This came for you, sir. Special delivery, from Alice Springs. Probably something you purchased there, sir, too heavy and cumbersome to carry with you on your flight."

"Probably," said Grimes. "But I'll catch up with my mail, Mr. Steerforth, before I unpack it. I'll yell for you as soon as I'm through."

"Very good, sir."

His curiosity unsatisfied, Steerforth left the cabin. He said to Shirl and Darleen, who were about to enter with Grimes' baggage, "Report to me as soon as the captain's finished with you."

Shirl said, "I liked Billy Williams."

Darleen said, "So did I."

Grimes said, "Billy Williams earned his long service leave. And try to remember, young ladies, that when you knew Billy Williams you were passengers in this ship, and privileged. Now you are very junior officers and Mr. Steerforth is a senior officer, my second in command. Meanwhile, I still have a job for you. To help me unpack this."

Like most spacemen he always carried on his person a multi-purpose implement that was called, for some forgotten reason, a Swiss Army Knife. (Once Grimes had asked his father about it and had been told that there was, a long time ago, a Swiss Army and that a special pocketknife had been invented for the use of its officers, incorporating a variety of tools, so that they would never lack the means to open a bottle of wine or beer.)

Anyhow, Grimes' pocket toolchest had a suitable screwdriver. He used it while Shirl and Darleen held the long box steady. At last he had all the securing screws out of the lid and gently pried it away from the body of the case, put it to one side on the deck. And then there was the foam plastic packing to be dealt with. He knew what he would find as he pulled it away.

She stood there in her box, her transparent skin glistening, the ornamental complexity of shining wheels on their jeweled pivots motionless. And he stood there looking at her, hesitant. He knew the simple procedure for activation—but should he?

Why not?

He inserted the index finger of his right hand into her navel, pressed. He heard the sharp click. He saw the transparent eyelids—a rather absurd refinement!—open and a faint flicker of light in the curiously blank eyes. He saw the wheels of the spurious clockwork mechanism begin to turn, some slowly, some spinning rapidly. There was a barely audible ticking.

The lips moved and. . . .

"Hello, sailor," said Seiko seductively.

"Mphm," grunted Grimes. Then, gesturing toward the litter of foam packing, "Get this mess cleaned up."

Shirl and Darleen laughed.

"Now there's somebody else to do the fetching and carrying!" said one of them.

Grimes dealt with his mail while Seiko busied herself with what Grimes thought was quite unnecessary dusting and polishing. There was a letter from his father, written before Grimes had left the family home to return to his ship. *I don't like the idea of returning Seiko to the makers,* the old man had written. *They'd take her apart to find out what went wrong—or went right!—and when they put her together again she'd be no more than just another brainless robomaid with no more intelligence than a social insect. And she would, of course, lose her personality. I'm hoping that*

*you'll be able to use her aboard your ship, as
your personal servant. . . .*

Then there was a brief note from Admiral
Damien, inviting him—or ordering him—to dinner in the admiral's own dining room that evening.

He was interrupted briefly by his new catering
officer, Melinda Clay. He looked up at her ap-
provingly. She was a tall woman, of the same
race as Cleo Jones, the radio officer, and Cassandra
Perkins, the fourth RD engineer. She was at least
as beautiful as Cleo, although in a different way.
The hair of her head was snowy white, in vivid
contrast to the flawless black skin of her face.
Natural or artificial? Grimes wondered.

"I came up, sir," she said, "to introduce myself. . . ."

"I'm very happy to have you aboard, Ms. Clay,"
said Grimes, extending his hand.

She shook it, then went on, "And to find out,
before the voyage starts, if you have any special
preferences in the way of food and drink. That
way I can include such items in my stores."

"Unluckily," laughed Grimes, "my very special
preferences are also very expensive—and as owner,
as well as master, I should have to foot the bill.
Just stock up normally. And I'm quite omnivorous.
As long as the food is good, I'll eat it. . . ."

Seiko came out of the bathroom, where she had
been giving the shower fittings a thorough polishing.

Melinda's eyes widened. "What a lovely robot! I didn't know that you carried your own robo-maid."

"I didn't know myself until I unpacked her. She's a gift, from my father."

"*She*? But of course, sir. You could hardly call such a beautiful thing it."

"Seiko," said Grimes, "this is Ms. Clay, my catering officer. When you are not looking after me—and I do not require much looking after—you will act as her assistant."

"Your father's last instructions to me, sir," said Seiko, "were that I was to be your personal servant."

"And *my* instructions to you," said Grimes firmly, "are that you are to consider yourself a member of the domestic staff of this vessel. Your immediate superior is Ms. Clay."

"Yes, Massa."

"Seiko, you are not supposed to have a sense of humor."

Melinda Clay laughed. "Don't be so serious, captain! I'm sure that Seiko and I will get on very well."

A slave and the descendant of slaves . . . thought Grimes wryly.

Chapter 9

Damien had another dinner guest, a tall, severely black-clad, gray-haired woman, with classic perfect features, who was introduced to Grimes as Madam Duvalier, First Secretary of the Aboriginal Protection Society. Grimes had already heard of this body, although it was of quite recent origin. It had been described in an editorial in *The Ship Operators' Journal*, to which publication Grimes subscribed, as an organization of trendy do-gooders obstructing honest commercial progress. And there had been cases, Grimes knew, where the APS had done much more harm than good. Their campaign on behalf of the down-trodden Droogh, for example.... The Droogh were one of the two sentient races inhabiting a world called Tarabel,

an Earth-type planet. They were a sluggish, reptil-
ian people, living in filth, literally, because they
liked it, practicing cannibalism as a means of
population control, fanatically worshipping a de-
ity called The Great Worm who could be dis-
suaded from destroying the Universe only by
regular, bloody sacrifices of any life-form unlucky
enough to fall into Droogh clutches. The other
sentient race on Tarabel had been the Marmura,
vaguely simian, although six-limbed beings. It was
with them that the first Terran traders had dealt,
taking in exchange for manufactured goods, including firearms, bales of tanned Droogh hides. It
was learned later—too late—that, at first, these
hides had been the left-overs from the Droogh
cannibal feasts. A little later many of the hides
had come from Droogh who had been killed, by
machine gun fire, when mounting unprovoked
attacks on Marmuran villages, the purpose of
which had been to obtain raw material for blood
sacrifices to The Great Worm.

Somebody in the Walk Proud Shoe Factory just
outside New York had become curious about obvious bulletholes in Droogh hides and had gone to
the trouble of getting information about Tarabel
and had learned that the Droogh were sentient
beings. Then APS had gotten into the act. A SAVE
THE DROOGH! campaign was mounted. Pressure
was exerted upon the Bureau of Extraterrestrial
Affairs. A Survey Service cruiser was dispatched

to Tarabel, not to investigate (which would have
made sense) but to disarm the Marmura. This was
done, although not without loss of life on both
sides. Then the cruiser was called away on some
urgent business elsewhere in the galaxy.

The next ship to make planetfall on Tarabel
was a Dog Star Line tramp. Her captain did not
get the expected consignment of Droogh hides—
and, in any case, there weren't any Marmura for
him to trade with. In the ruins of the small town
near the primitive spaceport were several Droogh.
These tried to interest him in a few bales of badly
tanned, stinking Marmura skins. He was not interested and got upstairs in a hurry before things
turned really nasty.

And the Droogh were left to their own, thoroughly unpleasant, devices.

Grimes remembered this story while he, the
admiral and Madame Duvalier were sipping their
drinks and chatting before dinner. Somehow the
conversation got around to the problem of primitive aborigines introduced to modern technology,
of how much interference with native cultures
was justifiable.

"There was the Tarabel affair . . ." said Grimes.

The woman laughed ruefully.

"Yes," she admitted. "There was the Tarabel
affair." She extended a slim foot shod in dull-
gleaming, grained, very dark blue leather. "You
will note, captain, that I have no qualms about

wearing shoes made of Droogh hide. I know, now, that the late owner of the skin was either butchered by his or her own people for a cannibal feast or shot, in self defense, by the Marmura. We, at APS, should have been sure of our facts before we mounted our crusade in behalf of the Droogh.

"But tell me—and please be frank—what do you really think of people like ourselves? Those who are referred to, often as not, as interfering do-gooders. . . ."

Rear Admiral Damien laughed, a rare display of merriment, so uninhibited that the miniature medals on the left breast of his mess jacket tinkled.

"Young Grimes, Yvonne," he finally chuckled, "is the do-gooder of all do-gooders, although I've no doubt that he'll hate me for pinning that label on him. He's always on the side of the angels but, at the same time, contrives to make some sort of profit for himself."

Madame Duvalier permitted herself a faint smile. "But you still haven't answered my question, captain. What do you think of do-gooders? Organized do-gooders, such as APS."

"Mphm." Grimes took a large sip from his pink gin, then gained more time by refilling and lighting his pipe. "Mphm. Well, one trouble with do-gooders is that they, far too often, bust a gut on behalf of the thoroughly undeserving while ignoring the plight of their victims. They seem, far too often, to think that an unpopular cause is automatically a just cause. Most of the time it isn't. But, on the other hand, anybody backed by big business or big government is all too often a bad bastard. . . ."

"He may be a son of a bitch," contributed Damien, "but he's our son of a bitch."

"Yes. That's the attitude far too often, sir."

"And so, young Grimes, you're interfering, as a free-lance do-gooder, every time that you get the chance."

"I don't interfere, sir. Things sort of happen around me."

"Captain Grimes," said Damien to Madame Duvalier, "is a sort of catalyst. Put him in any sort of situation where things aren't quite right and they almost immediately start going from bad to worse. And then, when it's all over but the shouting—or, even, the shooting—who emerges from the stinking mess, smelling of violets, with the Shaara crown jewels clutched in his hot little hand? Grimes, that's who. And, at the same time, virtue is triumphant and vice defeated."

Grimes's prominent ears flushed. Was the Duvalier female looking at him with admiration or amusement?

The sound of a bugle drifted into Damien's sitting room—which could have been the admiral's day cabin aboard a grand fleet flagship. (Damien was a great traditionalist.) Damien got to his feet, extended an unnecessary hand to Madam Duvalier to help her to hers. He escorted the lady into the dining room, followed by Grimes.

The meal, served by smartly uniformed mess waiters, was pleasant enough although, thought Grimes, probably he would have fed better aboard his own ship. But in *Sister Sue* it was *his* tastes that were catered to, here, in Flag House, it was Damien's. The admiral liked his beef well done, Grimes liked his charred on the outside and raw on the inside. Even so, Grimes admitted, the old bastard knew his wines, the whites and the reds, the drys and the semi-sweets, each served with the appropriate course. But it was a great pity that whoever had assembled the cheese board had been so thoroughly uninspired.

During dinner the conversation was on generalities. And then, with the mess waiters dismissed, Damien and his guests returned to the sitting room for coffee (so-so) and brandy (good) and some real talking.

"Yvonne," said the admiral, "is one of the very few people who knows that you are back in the Survey Service, as a sort of trouble shooter. She thinks that you may be able to do some work for APS."

"Since the Tarabel bungle," the woman admitted, "APS doesn't have the influence in high government circles that it once did. But there are still wrongs that need righting, and still powerful business interests putting profits before all else. . . ."

"And how can I help?" asked Grimes. "After all, I represent a business interest myself, Far Traveler Couriers. Unless I make a profit I can't stay in business. And if I go broke I just can't see the Survey Service taking me back into the fold officially. . . ."

"Too right," murmured Damien.

"And I couldn't get into any of the major shipping lines without a big drop in rank. I don't fancy starting afresh as a junior officer at my age."

"Understandable," murmured Damien. "And I hope that you understand that you need the Survey Service, even though you are, in the eyes of most people, a civilian, and a rich shipowner."

"Rich!" interjected Grimes. "Ha!"

"Just try to remember how much of your income has been derived from lucrative business that we have put in your way. All the charters, time or voyage. Such as the one that you have now, the shipment of not very essential and certainly not urgently required stores to the sub-base on Pleth."

"And after Pleth? What then?"

"Arrangements have been made. It will just so happen that there will be a cargo offering from Pleth to New Otago. Pleth exports the so-called paradise fruit, canned. Have you ever sampled that delicacy?"

"Once," said Grimes. "I wasn't all that impressed. Too sweet. Not enough flavor."

"Apparently the New Otagoans like it. Now, listen carefully. Your trajectory will take you within spitting distance of New Salem. What do you know of Salem?"

"I've never been there, sir, but I seem to remember that it's famous for the animal furs, very expensive furs, that it exports. Quite a few of the very rich bitches on El Dorado like to tart themselves up in them. Oh, yes. And this fur export trade is the monopoly of Able Enterprises. . . ."

"Which outfit," said Damien, "is run by old cobber Commodore Baron Kane, of El Dorado."

"No cobber of mine," growled Grimes.

"But you know Kane. And you know that any enterprise in which he's involved is liable to be, at the very least, unsavory. Well, APS have heard stories about this fur trade. APS have asked me to carry out an investigation. After all, I'm only a rear admiral. But I have clashed, in the past, with the El Dorado Corporation and gotten away with it. . . ."

"With me as your cat's-paw," said Grimes.

"Precisely. And, admit it, it does give you some satisfaction to score off Kane. Doesn't it?"

"I suppose so."

"It does, and we both know it." He turned to

Madame Duvalier. "Grimes and Kane are old enemies," he explained. "Apart from anything else there was rivalry for the favors of the Baroness Michelle d'Estang, who is now Kane's wife—hence his El Doradan citizenship."

Then, speaking again to Grimes, he went on, "I wanted to send a Survey Service ship to Salem on a flag-showing exercise but there just aren't any ships available. So I have to fall back on you."

"Thank you. Sir." Then, "But I shan't be bound for Salem."

"Officially, no. But look at it this way. You are bound from Point A to Point C, by-passing Point B. But then, in mid-voyage, something happens that obliges you to make for a port of refuge to carry out essential repairs or whatever. . . ."

"What something?" demanded Grimes.

"Use your imagination, young man."

"Mphm. . . . A leakage, into space, of my water reserves. . . . And, after all, water is required as reaction mass for my emergency rocket drive as well as for drinking, washing, etc. And so I get permission from the Salem aerospace authorities to make a landing, fill my tanks and lift off again. But I shall be on the planetary surface for a matter of hours only."

"Not if your inertial drive goes seriously on the blink just as you're landing."

"I'm not an engineer, sir, as well you know."

"But you have engineers, don't you? And among them is a Ms. Cassandra Perkins. Calamity Cassie."

"What do you know about her, sir?"

"I know that Lieutenant Commander Cassandra Perkins is an extremely skillful saboteur—or should that be saboteuse?"

"So she's one of your mob. . . ."

"And your mob, Captain Grimes. Federation Survey Service Reserve."

"All right. So I'm grounded on Salem for some indefinite period. And I suppose that I shall be required to do some sniffing around. . . ."

"You suppose correctly."

"Then why can't you do as you did before, give me one of your psionic communication officers, a trained telepath, to do the snooping? You will recall that I carried your Lieutenant Commander Mayhew, as an alleged passenger, when I was involved in the El Doradan privateering affair."

"At the moment, Grimes, PCOs are as scarce as hen's teeth in the Service. The bastards have been resigning in droves, recruited by various industrial espionage outfits. You may have heard of the war—yes, you could call it that—being waged by quite a few companies throughout the Galaxy against the so-called Wizards of Electra. But you have Shirl and Darleen who, despite their official human status, possess great empathy with the lower animals."

"And so, with the skilled assistance of your Ms. Perkins. . . ."

"*Your* Ms. Perkins, Grimes. She's on *your* books."

". . . I'm to prolong my stay on Salem as long as possible, find out what I can, and then write a report for you."

"Yes. And, hopefully, act as a catalyst. You always do."

"That's what I'm afraid of," said Grimes.

Yvonne Duvalier broke the brief silence.

She said, "I don't think that you have put Captain Grimes sufficiently into the picture, admiral. To begin with, captain, there was what Admiral Damien refers to as a flag-showing exercise on New Salem. The destroyer *Pollux*. She carried, of course, a psionic communication officer. He was not a very experienced one but he suspected, strongly, that at least one of the species of fur-bearing animal on New Salem, the silkies, possessed intelligence up to human standards. They can think and feel, but their thought processes aren't the same as ours. And they are slaughtered for their pelts. Somehow his not very detailed report fell into our hands, at APS. The admiral has long been a friend of ours and promised to do something about it. And then, as you know, there was the Tarabel fiasco and the consequent reluctance of the authorities to rush to the aid of unpleasant and vicious extra-Terrans.

"Although the fur of the silkies is beautiful, as you probably know, they are ugly beasts. They have, in the past, attacked the coastwise villages of the human colonists of New Salem. They have mutilated rather than killed, biting the hands off men, women and children. There are some rather horrid photographs of such victims.

"The New Salem colonists are the descendants of a religious sect that emigrated from Earth during the Second Expansion. Fundamentalists, maintaining that God gave Man dominion over all other life forms. They have their own version, their own translation of the Holy Bible, the Old Testament only. Their God is a jealous God, taking a dim view of any who do not believe as the True Believers, as they call themselves, do. But they do not mind taking the money of those who are not True Believers. They have a huge account in the Galactic Bank, more than enough to pay for the occasional shipments of manufactured goods that they receive from the industrial planets. Popular belief is that, eventually, their funds will be used for the building of a huge Ark in which they, and they alone, will escape the eventual collapse of the Universe."

"Where will they escape to?" asked Grimes interestedly.

Damien laughed. "I don't suppose they know

themselves. Perhaps they just hope to drift around until the next Big Bang, and then get in on the ground floor and start the human race again the way it should be started, free of all perversions. . . ." Suddenly he looked at Grimes very keenly. "Talking of perversions, young man, I hear that you are perverting Survey Service Regulations."

"Me, sir?"

"Yes. You. The regulations regarding wild robots. I hear that you have one such aboard your ship. You have neither deactivated it and returned it to its makers nor destroyed it."

"I suppose that Mr. Steerforth told you, sir."

"Never mind who told me. I just know."

"I'd like to make it plain, sir, that my ship is my ship. I am the owner as well as the master. Until, if ever, she is officially commissioned as an auxiliary unit of the Survey Service she is a merchant ship. The regulations to which her personnel are subject are company's regulations. In this case, my regulations."

"Always the space lawyer, Grimes, aren't you?"

"Yes. I have to be."

Damien grinned. "Very well, then. I'll just hope that your Seiko, as I understand that you call the thing, will be just another catalyst thrown into the New Salem crucible. Two wild girls, one wild robot and, the wildest factor of all, yourself. . . ."

"I almost wish that I were going along on the voyage," said Madame Duvalier.

"Knowing Grimes as I do," said the admiral, "I prefer to wait for the reports that I shall be getting eventually. Reports which I shall not pass on to higher authorities until they have been most thoroughly edited."

Chapter 10

Sister Sue lifted from Port Woomera, driving up into the cloudless, blue, late afternoon sky. As members of the crew, Shirl and Darleen were among those in the control room; as first trip cadets their only duty was to keep well out of the way of those doing the work. Up and out drove the old ship, up and out. Soon, far to the south, the glimmer of the Antarctic ice could be discerned and, much closer, there was a great berg with its small fleet of attendant tugs, being dragged and nudged to its last resting place, its dying place, in the artificial fresh water harbor at the mouth of the Torrens River.

The sky darkened to indigo and the stars appeared, although the bright-blazing sun was still well clear of the rounded rim of the Earth. In the stern vision screen the radar altimeter display totted up the steadily increasing tally of kilometers. There were the last exchanges of messages between Aerospace Control and the ship on NST radio. It was a normal start to a normal voyage. (But, thought Grimes, sitting in his command chair, his unlit pipe clenched between his teeth, for him a normal voyage was one during which abnormality was all too often the norm. And, not for the first time, Damien was expecting him to stick his neck out and get it trodden on.)

Earth was a sphere now, a great, glowing opal against the black velvet backdrop of space.

"Escape velocity, sir," announced Harald Steerforth.

"Thank you, Mr. Steerforth," said Grimes.

"Clear of the Van Allens, sir," reported the second officer.

"Thank you, Mr. Kershaw. Ms. Suzuki, make to all hands 'Stand by for free fall. Stand by for trajectory adjustment.' "

He heard the girl speaking into her microphone, heard, from the intercom speakers the reports from various parts of the ship that all was secured. Using the controls set in the broad armrest of his chair he shut down the inertial drive. There was an abrupt cessation of vibration and a brief silence, broken almost at once by the humming of the great gyroscopes around which *Sister Sue* turned, hunting the target star. Grimes' fingers played on the control buttons, his face upturned to the curiously old-fashioned cartwheel sight set at the apex of the transparent dome of the control room. The pilot computer could have done the job just as well and much faster—but Grimes always liked to feel that he was in command, not some uppity robot. At last the tiny, bright spark was in the exact center of the concentric rings, the convergence of radii. It did not stay there for long; there was allowance for Galactic Drift to be made.

At last Grimes was satisfied.

"Stand by for initiation of Mannschenn Drive," he ordered.

"Stand by for initiation of Mannschenn Drive," repeated Tomoko Suzuki.

In the Mannschenn Drive room the gleaming complexity of rotors came to life, spinning faster and faster, tumbling, precessing, fading almost to invisibility, warping the very fabric of Space-Time about themselves and about the ship, falling down the dark dimensions. . . .

The temporal precession field built up and there was the inevitable distortion of perspective, with colors sagging down the spectrum. Not for the first time Grimes experienced a flash of prevision—but, he knew, it was of something that *might* happen. After all, there is an infinitude of possible futures and a great many probable ones.

But he saw—and this was by no means his first

such experience—a woman. It was nobody he knew—and yet she seemed familiar. She was clad in a dark blue, gold-embroidered kimono, above which her heavily made-up face was very pale. Her glossy, black hair was piled high on her head. She could almost have been a Japanese geisha from olden times. . . .

Tomoko? Grimes wondered.

No, she was not Tomoko.

He could see her more clearly now. She was bound to a stake, around which faggots were piled. He saw a hand, a human hand, apply a blazing torch to the sacrificial pyre. There were flames, mounting swiftly. There was smoke, swirling about and over the victim.

There was. . . .

There was the instantaneous reversion to normality as the temporal precession field was established. Grimes tried to shake the vision from his mind.

"Stand by for resumption of inertial drive," he ordered.

"Stand by for resumption of inertial drive," repeated Tomoko into her microphone.

From below came the muted arrhythmic thumping. Somewhere a loose fitting rattled. Grimes unsnapped his seat belt, took his time lighting and filling his pipe.

"Set normal Deep Space watches," he said to the chief officer. "Mr. Kershaw can keep the first one. Please join me in my day cabin for a drink before dinner, Mr. Steerforth. We've a few things to discuss."

"Thank you, sir."

"I take it," said Grimes, speaking over the rim of his glass, "that Admiral Damien has put you into the picture."

"Of course, sir."

"What do you know about Ms. Perkins? Or should I say Lieutenant Commander Perkins?"

"I've worked with her before, sir. I knew that she'd been planted in your ship some time ago. She's highly capable, masquerading as being highly incapable." Then Steerforth actually laughed. "Mind you, sir, I've often wondered if her masquerade *is* a masquerade. . . . Perhaps, like you, she's a sort of catalyst. Things just happen when she's around."

"Can she make them happen on demand?" asked Grimes.

"Usually," said Steerforth.

"Mphm. But tell me, Mr. Steerforth, just how many undercover agents has Admiral Damien planted aboard my ship?"

"Well, sir, there's you, for a start. And myself. And Ms. Perkins. And those two alleged officer cadets. . . ." After a couple of drinks he was becoming more human. "For all *I* know that clockwork toy of yours might even be one! Tell me, is she really intelligent? Or is she just an example of very clever programming on somebody's part?"

"We are all of us the end products of programming," Grimes told him.

"To a point, sir. To a point. But as well as the programming there's intuition, imagination, initiative. . . ."

"I think," said Grimes, "that Seiko possesses at least two of those qualities."

The dinner gong sounded.

The two men finished their drinks, went down to the wardroom to join the other off duty officers.

Grimes had been half expecting soul food but what Ms. Clay provided was a fine example of Creole cookery. This was not to everybody's taste but Grimes enjoyed it.

Chapter 11

It was not a long voyage to Pleth, but long enough for Grimes to get the feel of things. His new chief officer, Harald Steerforth, was not quite such a pain in the arse as Grimes had feared that he would be on first acquaintance. Cleo Jones, the black and beautiful radio officer, the Zulu Princess, was the civilizing influence. What the pair of them did when they were off watch was none of Grimes' business. These days, in vessels with mixed crews, temporary sexual unions were not discouraged so long as they did not interfere with the smooth running of the ship and so long as certain unwritten regulations were observed.

In fact, thought Grimes disgruntledly, about the only person who wasn't getting any was himself.

He was the victim of those unwritten regulations. Shirl and Darleen had made it plain to him that they were available, as they had been when they had traveled as passengers in *Sister Sue* from New Sparta to Earth. But then they had been passengers, fair game. Now they were junior officers, *very* junior officers. Between Grimes and themselves there was too great a disparity of rank. He did not wish to be thought of as a wicked captain who ordered poor, helpless (ha!) first-trip cadets to his bed.

Oh, there were offers, opportunities, but the two New Alicians did their best (worst) to ensure that he did not take advantage of them. There was that handsome academic, Sarah Smith, the second Mannschenn Drive engineer. She made it plain that she would not find the attentions of her captain unwelcome. Perhaps it was accidental that when she walked into the wardroom one evening, ship's time, she was struck on the left shoulder by a heavy glass ashtray. Shirl had been giving an exhibition of boomerang throwing—using anything and everything as boomerangs—to the off-duty officers.

Perhaps, Grimes thought at the time, it was accidental—but the next morning, in his day cabin, the two girls, who were supposed to be receiving instruction in general spacemanship from the captain, told him otherwise.

"John," said Shirl, "Vinegar Puss is trying to get her claws into you. Warn her off. . . ."

"Or next time," said Darleen, "she'll be getting something hard and heavy where it really hurts."

"And the same applies," added Shirl, "to Aunt Jemima. . . ."

"Ms. Clay," objected Grimes, "is nothing like Aunt Jemima."

"She's the cook, isn't she?"

"She's the catering officer," said Grimes. "It's the autochef that does the cooking—with, I admit, her personal touches. But Aunt Jemima? I've never heard her called that."

"You don't know much about what goes on aboard your own ship," Shirl told him.

Grimes laughed. "I'm only the captain. Nobody ever tells me anything."

"Then we can be your spies, John. You've made it plain that we aren't to be anything else."

"I've told you why it's quite impossible, as long as you're on my books."

"But it's so *silly*," complained the girls in unison.

"Silly or not, that's the way it's going to be."

"Would you rather that we slept with Bill the Bull?"

William Bull was the 3rd reaction drive engineer, the only male member of his department. He was referred to as "the bull among the cows." It was a known fact that both the 2nd and 4th were recipi-

ents of his favors. Privately Grimes thought of
him as a sullen, over-sexed lout.

He said, "I'd advise you not to. Juanita has a
hot temper and Calamity Cassie might put a hex
on you. Well, since you are now my self-appointed
spies, what else have you for me that you think
that I don't already know?"

"Tomoko. . . ."

"Ms. Suzuki to you. After all, she is your superior officer."

"Only just," said Shirl. "And only aboard this
ship of yours. Well, she and Seiko are very
friendly. They have long talks together, twittering
and giggling away in Japanese. Anyhow, we think
that it's in Japanese."

"It probably is," Grimes said. "Tomoko must
be pleased to have somebody with whom she can
chat in her native language. It's the one that was
originally programmed into her—Seiko, I mean,
although I suppose that you could say the same
regarding Tomoko."

"But Tomoko is not a robot," objected Darleen.

"Isn't she? Aren't you? Or, come to that, me?
We're all of us programmed, from birth onward."

"You are too deep for us, John. We are not
accustomed to such philosophical thinking. On
New Alice we led simple lives, at one with
Nature. . . ."

And this was so, Grimes knew. He had watched
Shirl and Darleen running with the mob of kanga-

roos by the Uluru Canal near Ayers Rock, heard
them talking to the marsupials. He knew that
aboard _Sister Sue_ the two girls were now practically in charge of the ship's hydroponic "farm,"
that even the various edible, tank-grown plants
flourished, under their care, as never before. They
had green fingers, declared Melinda Clay who, as
catering officer, was responsible for the continu-
ing supply of fresh fruits, salads and other vege-
tables.

So _Sister Sue_ eventually made her planetfall in
the vicinity of Pleth, emerged from the warped
continuum into normal space-time, said all the
right things to the planet's Aerospace Control, got
all the right answers and, eventually, dropped
through thick clouds, all the way from the strato-
sphere to the ground, to the spaceport. This, with
facilities capable of handling no more than two
ships at the one time, was shared by the Survey
Service and commercial interests. Grimes' berth
was marked not by the usual flashing red beacons
but by a radar transponder; it is said the visibility
is bad for nine months of the local year on Pleth
and nonexistent for the remaining three.

Grimes set his ship down gently, making, he
told himself, a very good job of it in these
conditions. He sat in the control room with
Steerforth after the others had left, looking out
through a viewport at ... nothing. At least he

knew which way to look; his radar, set on short range, showed him a blob of luminescence that probably indicated the port administration building.

He saw the gradually increasing yellow glare in the fog that came from the headlights of approaching ground vehicles. Ms. Clay, in her capacity as purser, would, he knew, have all the necessary ship's papers ready in her office. Ms. Suzuki would receive the boarding officers in the after airlock. His presence almost certainly would not be required. Customs, Port Health and Immigration would be getting their free smokes and coffee and then applying their rubber stamps before leaving.

Steerforth said, "I'd better get down to my office, sir. I suppose that somebody will be wanting to arrange discharge." He laughed. "I don't suppose that the Sub-Base Commander will be inviting us across for drinks."

That was indeed unlikely, thought Grimes. From his long experience he had learned that the smaller the Base, the greater the sense of self-importance of the officer in charge. On a planet like Pleth the OIC would most likely be some passed-over commander, putting on the airs and graces of a fleet admiral, too high and mighty to share a noggin of gin with a mere tramp skipper and his mate.

"I shall be in my day cabin if anybody wants me, Mr. Steerforth," he said. "Probably the agent will come aboard once the ship has been cleared inwards."

Shortly after Grimes had settled down in his day cabin with a mug of hot, sweet coffee to hand, his pipe drawing well, he was called upon by Mr. Klith, of Klith, Klith & Associates. Mr. Klith was obviously a native, although apparently humanoid. What could be seen of his skin was pale green and scaly and his huge eyes were hidden by even huger dark goggles, worn as protection from the relatively glaring illumination inside the ship. Although he wore a conventional enough gray, one-piece business suit his large, webbed feet were bare.

He spoke perfect, rather too perfect Standard English.

"I am your agent on Pleth, Captain," he announced. "Also I represent the Federation Survey Service, the consignees of your inward cargo."

"Sit down, Mr. Klith," said Grimes. "Can I offer you refreshment? Tea, coffee, something stronger? It is the middle of the morning your time, but I think that we can say that the sun is over the yardarm."

"We rarely see our sun," said Mr. Klith. "But what is a yardarm?"

"I must apologize," said Grimes. "I used an expression that used to be common at sea, on Earth, during the days of sail. It was passed on to mechanically driven ships and then to spaceships. It means that it's just about time for a drink before the midday meal."

"Thank you for your invitation, Captain. Perhaps I might have some tea. To us it is a mild intoxicant."

Grimes spoke briefly into the microphone of the intercom, turned to his guest. "What sort of tea would you prefer, Mr. Klith?"

"Indian tea is among our imports, Captain, but I understand that there are other varieties. I should wish to sample one of them."

Grimes amplified his order to the pantry.

"And now, Captain, while we are waiting might we discuss business?" said the agent. "I am afraid that we cannot expect much cooperation from Commander Dravitt, who is in charge of the Sub-Base. May I quote his words? He said, 'I need another load of bumf like I need a second arsehole. My stationery store is packed almost to bursting already.' But, you will be relieved to learn, I am the agent on this world for the Survey Service, not for one of its relatively junior—in rank, that is—officers. I have received a Carlottigram, signed by an Admiral Damien—do you know him, by any chance?—urging me to expedite your discharge. Your cargo will be stored in a civilian warehouse."

"As long as I'm not expected to pay for the storage," said Grimes.

"You will not be, Captain."

There was a tap at the door. Seiko came in, carrying a tray upon which were a teapot and a handleless cup. She set the tray down on the coffee table, poured the steaming fluid which almost matched Mr. Klith's skin in color. The native watched the robomaid with admiration, then transferred his attention to the refreshment.

He said, with some little bewilderment, "But should there not be sugar? And milk? Or perhaps some slices of that fruit you call lemon?"

"This is the way that we Japanese drink our tea, Klith-san," said Seiko.

"Indeed? But would not the ingestion of hot fluids tend to corrode your intricate and beautiful machinery?"

Grimes said hastily, "Seiko neither eats nor drinks. But she tends to identify with her manufacturers." Then, to the robot, "Thank you, Seiko. That will do."

"Thank you, Captain-san."

The robomaid withdrew.

"Your personal servant, Captain?" asked Mr. Klith. "A robot such as that must have been very, very expensive. All that we have on this world are clumsy things that are neither ornamental nor even very useful. But, of course, you are a rich shipowner and can afford the very best."

"Mphm," grunted Grimes. "As a matter of fact Seiko is a gift to me from my father. . . ."

"Then he must be a very rich man. Is he, too, in shipping?"

"No, he's a writer. . . ."

"Then he must be famous. Terran books are very popular here on Slith, both in translation and among those who, like myself, can read the various Terran languages. What name does he write under?"

Grimes told him.

"I am sorry. I have never heard of him. But he still must be successful and rich."

"Moderately successful and not really rich. As a matter of fact he bought Seiko for himself, to program as his secretary. That way he could claim her purchase price as a legitimate income tax deduction. Then my mother thought that she would make an ideal robomaid after secretarial skills somehow failed to develop, but she was still my father's pet. And then, after a family row, I got her. . . ."

"What complicated lives you Terrans lead. That is what makes your literature so fascinating. . . . This is excellent tea, by the way, captain. I must arrange to import it from Earth in large quantities . . ."

Grimes refiled his cup for him.

"And now, captain, let us discuss business. My young Mr. Slith is now with your chief officer discussing discharge of your inward cargo. This should commence shortly after noon, our time.

Our stowbots may not be as goodlooking as your robomaid but they are fast working, especially when no great care is required. . . ."

"Mr. Steerforth will make careful note of the marks and numbers of any packages damaged and I shall, of course, refuse to pay any claims for damaged cargo."

"As you please, captain. The Survey Service will just write off such claims. After all, it is by their insistence that your discharge will be an exceptionally speedy one. By tomorrow night you should have an empty ship. Loading will commence almost at once. You know, of course, that you will be carrying a cargo of paradise fruit to New Otago. . . ."

"Any need for refrigeration or special ventilation?"

"No. It is canned."

"Then I hope that some care is exercised in its loading. I don't want damaged crates and sticky juice dribbling all over my cargo decks."

"Due care will be exercised, Captain. Paradise fruit is our main export and we do not wish to antagonize our customers." He finished his tea and got to his feet. "Thank you for allowing me to sample this truly excellent brew."

"Aren't you staying for lunch?" asked Grimes, hoping that the answer would be negative. A little of Mr. Slith went a long way. Apart from anything else he exuded an odor of not very fresh fish. (*And what do I smell like to him?* wondered Grimes, making allowances.)

"No thank you, Captain. I must confess that I do not find Terran foods very palatable—apart from your tea, that is. But does that possess any nutritional value? And now I must be on my way. Business awaits me in my office."

"Before you go," asked Grimes, "can you tell me if there are any recreational facilities in Port Pleth? I always allow my people shore leave whenever possible."

"Alas, no. Had you come a few days earlier you could have witnessed our annual mud festival, an event in which I am trying to interest the operators of tourist liners, such as Trans-Galactic Clippers, so far without success. Too, it is unsafe for beings not blessed with our eyes, sensitive as they are to infra-red radiation, to wander through the town. A few months ago—as you reckon time— the second officer of a Dog Star Line vessel fell into the Murgh River and was drowned. . . ."

So, thought Grimes, he would have to announce that there was to be no shore leave. He did not think that anybody would object very strongly.

Chapter 12

But there was, after all, shore leave of a sort.

Just as Grimes was about to go down to the wardroom for his luncheon he had another caller, this one human, an ensign from the Sub-Base. This not-so-young (for his lowly rank he seemed quite elderly) gentleman handed Grimes a large, rather condescendingly but more or less correctly addressed envelope. *Commander John Grimes, FSS (Rtd.), Master dss Sister Sue.* (Grimes had held the rank of commander at the time of the *Discovery* mutiny but he had not been retired; he had resigned his commission in some haste.)

Inside the envelope was a stiff sheet of official Survey Service stationery. On it was typed, "Commander David Dravitt, Federation Survey Service,

Officer-in-Charge Sub-Base Pleth and his officers request the pleasure of the company of Commander John Grimes, Master dss *Sister Sue*, and his officers to dinner this evening, 1800 for 1930. Your prompt reply by bearer will be appreciated."

So far as he could remember Grimes had never been shipmates with Dravitt during his own days in the Service. He had never met, nor even heard of Dravitt. But, all too probably, Dravitt would have heard of him.

He asked, "Is there any limit to the number of guests, Mr. . . . Mr. . . . ?"

"Sullivan, sir. No, there is no limit. We enjoy commodious facilities. The Sub-Base was once much more important than it is now."

"Mphm. Can you handle fourteen, including myself?"

"Easily, sir. Will that be your entire complement?"

"No. Executive and engineer officers of the watch will remain on board. Will you be arranging transport?"

"It is only a short stroll to the Sub-Base officers' quarters, sir."

"In a thick fog, Mr. Sullivan?"

"We can lay on a ground car for yourself and your senior officers, sir. Native guides will be supplied for the others. The natives, as you may know, have eyes adapted to local conditions."

"Very well. You will call for us then at . . ."

"Shortly after 1730, sir."

"Thank you. Would you care to stay for lunch?"

Sullivan was obviously tempted but he said, "No thank you, sir. Commander Dravitt would like your reply as soon as possible so that the necessary arrangements may be made."

She, Paymaster Lieutenant Commander Selena Shaw, extricated herself from the tangle of bed sheets and limbs (half of these latter belonging to herself) and padded to the well-stocked bar set against one wall of her bedroom. Grimes watched the tall, naked blonde appreciatively. She returned to the bed bearing two condensation-bedewed glasses of sparkling wine.

"What," asked Grimes, "is a girl like you doing in a place like this? A highly competent officer attached to Sub-Base Pleth, the last resting place of all the Survey Service incompetents? Well, some of them, anyhow."

She laughed, her teeth very white in her tanned face. (She was one of the few officers of the Sub-Base who made regular use of the solarium; artificial sunlight was better than none at all.)

She said, without false modesty, "There has to be one competent officer, even in a sub-base like this. And I just happen to be it. Or her."

Grimes sipped his chilled wine. "And what am I," he continued rhetorically, "doing in a place like this? First of all, I never thought that a high

and mighty sub-base commander would condescend to entertain a mere tramp skipper. Secondly,
I was expecting a rather boring evening. I never
dreamed that it would finish up like this."

She said, "Actually the invitation was Droopy
Delia's idea. You've met her now, talked with
her, so your opinion of her probably coincides
with mine. A typical wife for a typical passed-
over commander, like Davy Dravy, swept with
him under the carpet to a dump like Pleth. Social
ambitions that will never now be realized. A
plumpish blonde—and now she's rather more than
plump—getting spliced to an ambitious young
lieutenant and seeing herself, after not too many
years, as an admiral's wife. An admiral's wife
she'll never be—but she kids herself that she's
running this sub-base. Shortly after you'd set down
she came barging into my office. *My* office, mind
you. Davy Dravy was there—well, after all he is
the sub-base commander—to discuss various matters and *she* started browsing through the papers
on *my* desk. 'David,' she squeaked, 'have you
seen who's master of this tramp, this *Sister Sue*?'
He grumbled back, 'What is it to me what star
tramp skippers call themselves?' She said, 'It's
Grimes. John Grimes. *The* Grimes.' Davy Dravy
was less than impressed. 'So bloody what?' he
snarled. 'He was emptied out of the Service, wasn't
he? And not before time.' She said, 'Yes. He was
emptied out of the Service—or, according to some,

he resigned before he could be emptied out. And now he's a shipowner. And he's been a planetary governor. At least he hasn't finished up with a dead-end appointment, frozen in rank, like some people.' Davy mumbled something about this being just your bloody luck. Droopy Delia said that she wished this famous luck would rub off on to some people she knew. And so it was decided to invite you to dinner. Or *she* decided to invite you to dinner. And then I took pity on you—or, as it's turned out, it was enlightened self-interest. Davy and Delia just aren't the Universe's best hosts. I threw in my two bits' worth. 'Why not,' I asked her, not him, 'issue a general wardroom invitation to the captain and officers. Our own officers, and the few civilian spouses, will enjoy having somebody fresh to talk with. . . .' "

"To talk with," said Grimes. "And. . . ."

"Yes. As you say, and as we've been doing, and . . . Apart from ourselves, I think that there has been rather more than just talking. But I don't think that Tony Cavallo and Billy Brown, our two prize wolves, got any place with those two cadets of yours. Odd looking wenches, somehow, but very attractive. And, despite their names, I don't think that their ancestors were Irish. I may be wrong, but I think that they had eyes only for you. And me, when I was making my invitation rather obvious. If looks could have killed. . . ."

"Mphm," grunted Grimes, embarrassed.

"Talking of their eyes. . . ." she went on. "Is there anything odd about *them*?"

"How do you mean?"

"Well, I was in charge of picking you people up and supplying the native guides for the junior officers. Your Ms. Kelly and Ms. Byrne arrived at the base officers' quarters well before the rest of the crowd—and they had nobody to guide them. And the fog was as thick as the armor plating of a Nova class battlewagon."

"Probably," said Grimes, "they regarded it as a sort of navigation test, got themselves headed in the right direction and then set off hopefully."

"Then they were lucky. It's not a straight line walk. There are two bridges to negotiate, and that mess of alleys and cross alleys through the workshops and stores."

"Mphm," grunted Grimes.

He finished his drink, she finished hers. It would soon be time for him to get back to his ship so as to spend what remained of the night in his own bed. But before he got dressed there were things to do better done naked.

At last it was time for him to say good night—or, more exactly, good morning. She threw on a robe and took him out to where the ground car, with native driver, was awaiting him.

He said, "I'll see you at about 1100 hours, then, Selena. Drinks before lunch. And I think I can

promise you a rather better meal than tonight's
dinner was."

She said, "It should be. Aboard your ship you're
the boss."

They kissed a long moment and he boarded the
waiting vehicle.

She arrived aboard *Sister Sue* shortly after 1100,
supported, almost carried, by Ensigns Cavallo and
Brown. She was dazed, bleeding profusely from a
deep cut on the forehead. The efficient Melinda
Clay was called upon to administer first aid and,
after some delay, the sub-base's medical officer
was in attendance.

At last Grimes was able to find out what had
happened.

Selena had decided to walk from the sub-base
to the ship, escorted through the fog by one of the
native guides. Suddenly, without warning, she
had been struck by a heavy missile. The guide
had run to the ship to fetch help.

"I suppose, sir, that it was our fault," said Ensign Cavallo unhappily. "We should not have
encouraged them. But, after all, sir, they're your
officers, aboard your ship. . . ."

"Encouraged them? How?"

"We came on board for morning coffee. In the
wardroom Ms. Kelly and Ms. Byrne were giving a
demonstration of throwing weapons, using ashtrays
and such, making them sail around and come

back to their hands. I asked if this technique would be effective over a distance. They said that it was. So we all went down to the after airlock, and Ms. Kelly threw a rather thick glass saucer of some kind into the fog. We expected that it would come back, but it didn't. . . ."

"Ms. Kelly," asked Grimes severely, "Ms. Byrne, is this true?"

"Yes, sir," replied Shirl innocently. "But we had no idea that there would be anybody out in the fog. After all, if Ms. Shaw had been making her approach by ground car we should have seen the glare of the headlights. . . ."

"And so, quite by chance," said Grimes, "your random missle inflicted grievous bodily harm on Lieutenant Commander Shaw—"

And with that he had to be content. He could prove nothing—and, even if he could, what could he do about it? Shirl and Darleen were essential— or so he had been told by Damien—to the success of his mission. Selena had been no more than a pleasant diversion.

Chapter 13

The work of discharge and then of loading went smoothly. Grimes was able during his time in port to return some of the hospitality which he and his people had received from the sub-base personnel. He kept a close watch on the Terrible Twins, a joint nickname which Shirl and Darleen had quite suddenly acquired, making no further attempt to entertain Selena Shaw aboard his ship. (But her own quarters were quite adequate for purposes of mutual entertainment and she did not, as she could quite well have done, put him off by complaining that she had a severe headache.)

And then, with cargo well stowed, with all necessary in-port maintenance completed, it was time to lift off. Nobody board the ship was sorry, even though there were a few (very temporarily) broken hearts both in the sub-base and aboard *Sister Sue*. Sleth was such a dismal planet. Even New Otago would be better. Even though there was a shortage of bright lights on that world the scenery was said to be quite spectacular and the atmosphere was usually clear enough for it to be appreciated.

So *Sister Sue* lifted, ungumming herself from the omnipresent mud that, despite the thrice daily deployment of high pressure hoses, inevitably crept over the spaceport apron. She clattered aloft through the fog, through the overcast, finally broke free into the dazzling sunlight while the last tenuous shreds of the Sleth atmosphere whispered along her pitted sides.

There was the usual trajectory setting routine, after which the old ship, her Mannschenn Drive running as sweetly as that Space-Time-twisting contraption ever ran, was falling down and through the warped dimensions toward the New Otago primary. Deep space watches were set and Grimes went down to his day cabin, asking Mr. Steerforth to join him there. As soon as the chief officer was seated and had been given a drink to nurse, served by the glittering Seiko, Grimes used the intercom to talk to the chief reaction drive engineer. "Ms. Scott, I've noticed that my shower is giving trouble. I almost got scalded this morning. Could you send Ms. Perkins up to fix it? She's off watch, isn't she?"

"I'll come myself, Captain. You know what Calamity Cassie's like."

"I do, Flo. But as fourth engineer she's supposed to be the ship's plumber. It's time that she started to earn her pay."

"Well, it's your shower, Captain. It's you that's going to get boiled or flash-frozen. . . ."

And so, after a wait of only a few minutes, Ms. Perkins presented herself, attired for work in overalls that had once been white but which now displayed a multitude of ineradicable grease stains, carrying a tunefully clinking tool bag. Only her teeth, which her cheerful grin displayed generously in her black face, were clean and very white.

"Sit down, Cassie," ordered Grimes.

Before she could do so Seiko produced, as though from nowhere, a towel which the robomaid spread over the upholstery of the chair. The fourth engineer looked admiringly at the beautiful automaton and murmured, "I'd love to have the job of taking you apart and putting you together again, honey."

"That'd be the Sunny Friday!" snapped Seiko.

"My father," said Grimes, "improved upon the original programming, making additions from his own vocabulary."

"And so Seiko," said Cassie, "is no more than a sort of mechanical parrot. That I will not believe.

She's as human as you or me." She grinned. "There are even rumors that you and she have a beautiful relationship."

"I am the captain's personal servant," said Seiko stiffly. "Just that and nothing more. Unfortunately a relationship of a carnal nature would not be possible."

Grimes' prominent ears flushed angrily.

He said, "That will do, Seiko. Just fetch Ms. Perkins a drink, will you?"

"Yassuh, Massa Grimes. One Foster's lager a-comin' up, Missie Perkins."

"And now, Ms. Perkins," said Grimes as soon as Seiko had left them, "have you decided upon how you will carry out your act of sabotage?"

"Yes, sir. It will be quite simple. A disastrous leakage from the main water tank into the reaction drive engineroom. The bulkhead will give way—an area of it will have been treated with Softoll—to give it its trade name—which, as you know loosens molecular bonds in any metal. According to my calculations the application will take twelve hours to produce the desired effect. When you let me know the day, sir, when you wish the accident to happen I shall apply the Softoll at 1000 hours, during my watch. The flood will happen at 2200 hours—again during my watch. I shall panic. My one motivation will be to get rid of all that water. After all, there's electrical machinery that could be damaged, and I might get drowned. I'll open the dump valves."

"Make sure, Cassie," Steerforth told her, "that you get into your emergency suit before you start getting rid of everything of a fluid nature in the engine room. After all, you'll be throwing out the atmosphere along with the bath water."

She grinned. "I look after my reputation. Things always happen around me, never to me."

Grimes asked, "But won't the cause of the so-called accident be obvious? Flo and Juanita aren't fools, you know."

She told him, "It will be put down to metal fatigue—and it won't be the first case of metal fatigue in this rustbucket."

"Are you referring to my ship?" asked Grimes stiffly. "It's bad enough to have you doing things to her without having to listen to you insulting her."

"Sorry, Captain. But unless you can think of some other kind of trouble that will force us to deviate to Salem, I shall have to do things to your ship. But I'll try to keep the damage down to a minimum." She finished her beer. "And now," she went on brightly, "shall I fix your shower for you?"

"No," said Grimes. "No, repeat and underscore, NO."

Chapter 14

Grimes, of course, knew what was going to happen, and when.

At 2145 hours he was in the control room, having a chat with the officer of the watch, Tomoko Suzuki. As he frequently did just this before retiring for the night the third officer did not suspect that anything was amiss or about to go so. The topic of conversation was such that he almost forgot his real reason for being there, which was to ensure that the Mannschenn Drive was shut down at the first sign of trouble in the inertial drive engineroom. The dumping of tons of water would mean that the mass of the ship would be suddenly and drastically reduced—and any change of mass while running under Mannschenn Drive could be, probably would be, disastrous. There were stories of vessels so afflicted being unable to re-enter normal Space-Time or being thrown back into the remote Past. Nobody *knew*, of course (except for the crews of those ships) but there had been experiments and there was a huge amount of theoretical data which Grimes could not begin to understand.

"Captain-san," Tomoko was saying, "I regard your Seiko as a friend. She may be a robot but she is, somehow, a real woman, a real Japanese woman." She giggled. "I have made up her face, like that of an olden time geisha, and put a wig upon her head, and dressed her in a kimono. . . ."

"I must see this some time," said Grimes.

He looked out through the viewport to the stars that were not points of light but vague, pulsating nebulosities. He heard the thin, high whine of the Drive as it engendered the temporal precession field, the warping of the continuum through which the ship was falling. He switched his attention to the control room clock. 2155:30 . . . 31 . . . 32 . . . Would that bulkhead blow *exactly* on time? Probably not. And would Calamity Cassie hit her alarm button as soon as the first trickle of water appeared? It could be just too bad if she didn't.

"Is something worrying you, Captain-san?" asked Tomoko.

"I shouldn't have had a second helping of Aunt

Jemima's jambalaya at dinner this evening," lied Grimes.

2159:01. . . .

He filled in time by playing with his pipe, stuffing the bowl with tobacco, making a major production of lighting it.

2200:00 . . .

"It would be rather pleasant," said Tomoko, "if some time we had a Japanese catering officer. . . ."

"I'm very fond of sashimi myself," said Grimes, "but I doubt if some of the others would care for raw fish."

2201:03 . . . 04 . . . 05 . . .

"Seiko has told me," said Tomoko, "that the preparation of sushi, sashimi and the like was in her original programming. And we have the carp in some of the algae tanks. Perhaps one night, just for a change, we could enjoy a sashimi dinner . . ."

2203:15 . . . 16 . . . 17

A red light suddenly sprang into being on the console of the inertial drive controls. An alarm klaxon uttered the beginnings of a squawk. Grimes' hand flashed up to the Mannschenn Drive console, knocked the main switch to the off position. The thin, high whine deepened to a rumbling hum, faded into silence. Colors sagged down the spectrum, perspective was impossibly distorted. Outside the viewports the stars changed, coalescing from furry blobs into hard points of light. But, below decks, the inertial drive was still hammering away although its clangor was almost drowned by the hooting alarms. And then it, too, fell silent. Throughout the ship all the lights went out but there was less than a second of darkness before the power cells cut in to the major domestic circuits.

Grimes had been expecting what happened and had secured himself in his chair. Tomoko was unprepared. With the inertial drive off, the ship was in free fall and some involuntary movement had pushed her up from her seat and she was drifting, making rather futile swimming motions, above Grimes' head. With his right hand he was just able to reach her ankle, pulled her down and then into the chair beside his.

"What happened, sir?" she gasped.

He said, "I suppose that somebody will eventually condescend to tell us."

"Why did you shut the Mannschenn Drive off, sir?"

He told her—but it was less than the whole truth—"There was, and is, trouble with the inertial drive. Which meant, as we've just found out, a sudden transition from a comfortable one G to free fall. There was the risk that the MD engineer on watch—Mr. Siegel, isn't it?—might blunder into the Drive and get himself turned inside out or something equally messy."

She said admiringly, "You thought very fast,

Captain-san. I hope that I can think as fast when I am a captain."

Grimes never minded flattery, especially when it came from a pretty girl, even though in this case it was unearned. He supposed that if he had not been on the alert he would have acted as he had done, but not as fast.

He said to Tomoko, "Buzz the ID room, will you? Ask them what the hell's going on."

After an interval she reported, "The intercom seems to be out of order, sir." (This was not surprising. The waterproofing of electrical systems is not considered necessary in spaceships.)

Steerforth pulled himself into the control room. He reported, almost cheerfully, "There's all hell let loose down there, sir. As far as I can gather the after bulkhead of the main fresh water tank suddenly ruptured, flooding the ID room." He laughed. "Of course, it would have to happen on Calamity Cassie's watch. Then, according to Flo, what Cassie should have done was to drain the water into the engineers' store and workshop space. But she went into a panic and opened the dump valves. . . ."

"It is indeed fortunate," said Tomoko, "that the captain shut down the Mannschenn Drive before the loss of mass."

"It is indeed fortunate, Ms. Suzuki," agreed Steerforth. "Perhaps it was just another example of his famous luck."

"Mphm," grunted Grimes, looking severely at his chief officer.

"Shall I go back down," asked that gentleman, "to try to find out the extent of the damage?"

"No, Mr. Steerforth. Engineers don't like control room ornaments getting into their hair when they're trying to cope with some kind of emergency. Ms. Scott will keep us informed in her own good time."

Kershaw, the second officer, made his entrance into the control room. *About bloody well time,* thought Grimes. *Doesn't the puppy know that there's an emergency?* After him came Shirl and Darleen. There was some excuse for them; they were not real spacepersons. Finally Cleo Jones, the Zulu Princess, put in her appearance.

She reported, "I have been checking the main Carlotti transceiver, sir. Should it be necessary I can get out a Mayday using the power available."

"Thank you, Ms. Jones." Grimes looked around at his assembled people. They looked back at him, obviously awaiting orders. Well, he'd beter start giving some.

"Ms. Kelly, Ms. Byrne," he said, "report to Ms. Clay. Probably there are matters in her department needing attention. When the ID cut out nothing was secured for free fall."

"Ay, ay, sir," said the girls smartly.

Grimes watched them go. They handled them-

selves in the absence of gravity better than many
a seasoned spaceman.

"Mr. Kershaw, since the intercom seems to be
out of action you can report to Ms. Scott, to act as
runner to carry messages to me from her."

And she'll probably chew his ears off, he
thought, with some satisfaction.

"Shall I find out what's happened to Seiko,
sir?" asked Tomoko. "She might have been hurt.
Damaged, I mean. . . ."

Not her, thought Grimes. He said, "She is a
member of Ms. Clay's department. Probably she
is helping her to get things cleaned up."

"Do you wish to send any messages, sir?" asked
Cleo.

"Eventually," Grimes told her. "But I want to
know what I'm talking about before I start talking."
Then, to the third officer, "Get me a fix, will you?
The navigational equipment is on the emergency
circuit."

The girl busied herself at the chart tank, taking
bearings from three conveniently located Carlotti
Beacon Stations. Grimes unbuckled himself from
his chair, pulled himself to a position beside her.
He looked down into the simulation of the black-
ness of interstellar space, at the intersection of
the three glowing filaments, at the other filament
this was the extrapolation of *Sister Sue's* trajectory.
At right angles to this, close, was the brilliant
spark that was a star.

Grimes pointed the stem of his pipe at it.

"That sun?" he asked. "I may need to find a planet, one where there is fresh water available."

She punched computer keys, read out from the screen, "Salema, sir, so called by the people of its own habitable planet, which is variously known as Salem or New Salem. Catalogue number. . . ."

"Never mind that. And the people? Of Terran origin, aren't they?"

She punched more keys. "Yes, sir. Second Expansion stock."

"Now get that tin brain to do some sums for me. Running at a steady one G, with standard temporal precession, how long from here to planetfall?"

"As from now, sir, six days, fourteen hours and forty-five minutes."

"Mphm. We can survive that long on what water is left in the system, with rationing and recycling. There shouldn't be any need to go thirsty or get really dirty."

"Couldn't we carry on to New Otago, sir?"

"I'd not like to risk it. And I was brought up in the Survey Service, as you know, Tomoko. We always liked to have plenty of reaction mass on hand so that we could use emergency rocket drive if we had to. So I think that a deviation to New Salem is justified. The insurance should cover it."

And if it doesn't, he thought, *some Survey Service secret fund will be used to compensate me.*

From below decks came the whine of a generator starting up. Lights flickered and then brightened as the emergency circuit cut out and the main circuit cut in. Steerforth said, "Flo seems to be getting things under control. I wonder why she hasn't sent Mr. Kershaw up to keep us informed."

Kershaw pulled himself into the control room. "Sir, Ms. Scott isn't very communicative. So I checked up in the Mannschenn Drive room. The MD engineers are standing by, waiting to start up as soon as they have the power. Mr. Gray asked me to tell you that there is no damage."

"Thank you."

Finally Florence Scott made her appearance. Her once-white overalls were sweat-soaked and grease-stained, and more grease marked her broad, ruddy face.

"Captain," she announced, "we'll have the phones working again in a couple o' minutes but I thought I'd report the situation in person, not through your messenger boy." Kershaw flushed and scowled. "As ye already know, the engineroom got flooded. Anybody'd think that this was some tramp steamer on Earth's seas way back in the twentieth century, old style. Cassie didn't think; all she wanted to do was to get rid of all that water in a hurry. She could ha' let it drain into the store and workshop flat—but no. Not her. She opened the dump valves.

"There's nothing wrong with the innies that a little minor rewiring won't fix. I should be able to restart in half an hour. An' then you can restart the time twister an' we can be on our way. You may as well restart it now."

"What about fresh water?" asked Grimes.

"Enough. We'll not die o' thirst or go unwashed as long as we're careful."

"What about the emergency reaction drive?"

"There's no reaction mass. But emergency reaction drive was phased out years ago in the merchant service. It's not required by law."

Grimes said, "I may be old-fashioned, but I like to know that I have rockets under my arse should I feel the need for them in a hurry. I'm deviating to the nearest port of refuge, which is on New Salem. There we'll get the bulkhead patched and refill the tank."

"A needless expense and waste of time," sneered the chief engineer. "Oh, well, you're the captain."

"And the owner," Grimes reminded her firmly.

Chapter 15

There was Aerospace Control on New Salam, although its name was somewhat misleading. There was no aerial traffic, either lighter than or heavier than air, in the planet's atmosphere. ("If God had meant us to fly He would have given us wings.") But at Port Salem there was a Carlotti radio station with rather limited range and also an NST transceiver. Grimes got in touch while he was still proceeding toward the planet under Mannschenn Drive, using his Carlotti radio. This was an unusually troublesome procedure. According to the data in *Sister Sue's* library bank New Salem Aerospace Control maintained a listening watch for the first five minutes of every hour, daylight hours only and never on Sunday. The first time that Cleo Jones tried to get through it must have been Sunday on New Salem. During the next twenty-four-hour period, ship's time, the trouble was trying to get the ship's clocks synchronized with those at the spaceport. Finally Cleo arranged for a continuous automatic transmission with an alarm to sound as soon as there was a reply.

Grimes happened to be in the control room when this happened.

An irritable female voice came from the Carlotti speaker. "Port Salem Aerospace Control to unknown vessel. Identify yourself. Pass your message."

"*Sister Sue* to Port Salem," said Grimes. "Request permission to land to effect essential repairs."

"Stand by, *Sister Sue*. I shall come back to you."

Grimes stood by for a long time, having his lunch, served by the faithful Seiko, in the control room. At last the speaker crackled into life.

"Port Salem to *Sister Sue*. What is the nature of the repairs that you will require? I must warn you that our workshop facilities are limited."

"The patching of a ruptured bulkhead," said Grimes. "My own engineers can carry out the work as long as suitable plating is available. The replenishment of my fresh water supply."

"Stand by, *Sister Sue*."

There was another long wait.

Finally, "Materials will be made available to you. Fresh water will be obtainable from Lake Beulah. What is your ETA please?"

Clocks and calendar were synchronized and Grimes was able to give day and time for his return to the normal continuum and, not too approximately, for his eventual setting down at Port Salem.

Eventually *Sister Sue* was dropping through the twilight towards the huddle of yellowish lights that was New Salem. He would have preferred to have made a dawn approach but, after all, he was supposed to be in some sort of distress and, therefore, in some sort of hurry. The traffic control officer, whose sour featured face was visible in the screen of the NST radio transceiver, instructed him to set down in the center of the triangle formed by the berth markers. *What berth markers?* Grimes asked himself irritably. What did they use for berth marking beacons on this benighted planet? Candles? He stepped up magnification and definition in the stern vision screen. At last he saw them as he continued his cautious descent, three feeble, ruddy sparks.

He hoped that Cassandra Perkins fully understood what was expected of her. If she acted too soon, clumsily (but on purpose) tripping over her own feet and clutching at a lubrication line for support, bending it but not breaking it, throttling

the supply of oil to the governor bearings, Sister
Sue would fall for far too many meters, damaging
herself irreparably. The governor would have to
seize up almost immediately after Grimes applied
that final surge of thrust to cushion the landing.

He watched the read-out of the radar altimeter.
10 meters . . . 9 . . . 8 . . . 7 . . . 6 . . .

Now!

The cacophony of the inertial drive rose from
little more than an irritable mutter to an angry
clangor—then abruptly ceased. Sister Sue dropped
like a stone, a very large and heavy stone. Shock
absorbers screamed rather than sighed. Loose fittings rattled and there was a tinkling crash as
something tore adrift from its securing bolts.
Grimes slowly filled and lit his pipe—but even
though he had been expecting the accident it was
hard to maintain the pose of imperturbability.
Tomoko, he thought, to whom it had all come as
a big surprise, was making a far better job of it
than he was.

Steerforth voiced what must have been the
thought of all those in the control room.

"That's fucked it!" he said.

"Mr. Steerforth, mind your language," Grimes
told him.

The intercom speaker crackled and then Florence Scott's voice came from it. "ID room to
captain. Chief engineer here. The bearings of the

governor seem to have seized up. I am making an
immediate check of the extent of the damage."

"Thank you," Ms. Scott," said Grimes into his
microphone.

"MD room to captain." This was the chief
Mannschenn Drive engineer, Daniel Grey. "You
seem to have made a crash landing." *A blinding
glimpse of the obvious*, thought Grimes. "The jolt
unseated numbers one, three and four rotors from
their bearings. . . ."

Worse and worse, thought Grimes. *Or better
and better?*

"Apart from anything else," Grey went on, "the
Drive will have to be recalibrated once it has
been reassembled."

"Somebody's coming out to us, sir," announced
Steerforth.

Grimes got up from his chair, went to stand
with the chief officer by the viewport. He saw the
group of bobbing lights—hand-held lanterns?—and
the dimly illumined human forms.

He said, "Looks like a boarding party of some
kind. You'd better go down to the after airlock to
receive them. I shall be in my day cabin. Oh, on
your way down give Ms Clay my compliments
and tell her to keep Seiko out of sight as long as
there are any locals aboard."

Steerforth grinned. "Aunt Jemima's read that
article too, just as we all have. But *Star Scandal's*
not quite in the same class as the *Encyclopaedia*

Galactica, is it, sir? And their star reporter, Fenella
Pruin, never lets facts get in the way of a sensa-
tional story."

"Ms. Pruin," said Grimes, "is a very able inves-
tigative reporter."

"Oh, yes. You know her, sir. I was forgetting."

"We know her, too," said Shirl and Darleen as
one, making it plain that they held Fenella in
quite high regard.

In his day cabin Grimes picked up the rather
tattered copy of *Star Scandals* from the coffee
table. It would be advisable, he thought, to get it
out of sight before the visitors arrived. That lurid
cover, with its colored photograph of a naked
girl, chained to a stake and with flames licking
around her lower body . . . It had been the third
ID engineer, Bill the Bull, who had found this
particular issue of *Star Scandals* in his well-
thumbed collection of that pornographic, as often
as not, publication. As soon as it was known that
Sister Sue was deviating to Salem, Fenella's piece
on that planet had become almost required reading by all hands.

Fenella had visited Salem as a passenger aboard
Wombat, owned by Able Enterprises. (This, of
course, had been before she had gotten into the
bad books of Baron Kane, whose company Able
Enterprises was.) She had found it hard to sniff
out anything really juicy on Salem; the people

lived lives of utterly boring sexual probity. She had witnessed a slaughter of the silkies, the animals whose furs were Salem's only export—but Fenella was not at her best (worst?) as a writer on humanitarian issues. She blew up the business of her dancing dolls to absurd proportions. These tiny, beautifully made automata, one male, one female, not only danced to tinkling music but stripped, and when naked went through the motions of coitus. All very amusing to those of a kinky bent. . . .

Grimes read, "That party, in *Wombat's* wardroom, was inexpressably dreary. Pastor Coffin and his wife would drink only tea and insisted that this be both weak and tepid. In deference to the sensibilities of their guests Captain Timson and his officers did not smoke. Daringly I lit a cigarillo and was told, by the she-Coffin that if God had meant me to smoke He would have put a chimney on top of my head. I said that She had more important things to occupy Her time. This did not go down at all well.

"The conversation, such as it was, got on to the topic of machinery. Machinery, I gathered, was disapproved of on Salem. Of course I had already noticed this. Just one solar power plant to generate electricity for the spaceport facilities, communications and so forth. But oil-lighting in the houses, sailing vessels on the sea, bullock-drawn wagons on the roads. And bullocks, too, supplied the power to operate the presses which extracted the flammable oil from various seeds.

"Anyhow, Captain Timson was letting Pastor Coffin's diatribe against inventions of the devil go on without interruption. He knew on which side his bread was buttered. The silkie skin trade was a profitable one for his owners. But his officers, the engineers especially, were inclined to argue. The fruit punch that they had been drinking had been well spiked with gin as soon as it became obvious that the Coffin couple was having none of it.

"Terry Muldoon, the third engineer, said, 'But machines have their uses, Pastor Coffin. Even as toys for children, educational toys . . .' (Terry, I learned later, had already resigned from Able Enterprises and had a job waiting for him with the Dog Star Line.) Coffin said, 'What can a child learn from a mechanical toy? He will learn all that he ever needs to know from the Bible.' Terry said, 'You'd be surprised, Pastor.' He turned to me and said, 'Fenella, why not show our guests those educational toys of yours?' (He was one of the few people aboard the ship who had seen them. Old Timson had not, neither had the two chief engineers.) So I went to my cabin and got the box and set it down on the wardroom table. I took out Max and Maxine. They stood stiffly, facing each other. I switched on the music, Ravel's *Bolero*. Max and Mazine came . . . alive. They could have been flesh-and-blood beings, not automata. They danced, and as they danced they shed their clothing. I always liked the part when Max got rid of his trousers; it is easy for a woman to disrobe gracefully to music, not so easy for a man. I always hoped that Max would get his feet tangled in his nether garments and come down heavily on his rather too perfect little arse, but he never did.

' And then they were quite naked, the pair of them, anatomically correct. Maxine, legs open, was supine on the table top and Max was about to lower himself upon her when Coffin's big fist smashed down on the box as he bellowed, 'Blasphemy! Blasphemy!' The music stopped in mid-stridency. There was a sputter of sparks. Max, no more than a lifeless, somehow pathetic doll collapsed on top of the other doll, among the litter of rags that had been their clothing.

"Timson apologized. 'I had no idea, Pastor . . .'

"Coffin—he was virtually foaming at the mouth—screamed, 'That is no excuse, Captain. Does it not say in the Book that you shalt not suffer a witch to live? She . . .' he pointed a quivering finger at me, 'is a witch. And those are her familiars!'

" 'Go to your cabin,' Timson ordered me. I tried to argue but it was no use. The mate and the second mate, that pair of great, hulking louts, hustled me out of the wardroom, locked me in my quarters. And there I was confined until breakfast the next morning.

"After the meal Terry managed to have a few words with me. He told me that the pastor had gone on ranting and raving after I had been removed from his presence, accusing me of witchcraft and saying that Max and Maxine were my familiars. He demanded that I be turned over to the local authorities to stand trial—but this was too much even for Captain Timson. Then he insisted that Max and Maxine be given into his custody, saying that they would be publicly destroyed by burning. Timson agreed to this. 'And you'd better stay aboard from now on, Fenella,' Terry told me, 'otherwise you'll find yourself tied to a stake with the faggots piled about you . . .' "

There was a knock at the door. Grimes hastily took the dog-eared copy of *Star Scandals* through to his bedroom, returned to the day cabin and called, "Come in!"

Tomoko entered, followed by a tall man in rusty black clothing with touches of white, rather grimy white, at his throat and wrists.

"Pastor Coffin to see you, sir," she announced.

Grimes almost said what he usually said on such occasions but decided against it. To judge from the deeply lined, craggy face, the fanatical black eyes under shaggy gray brows, this was a man utterly devoid of humor.

Chapter 16

The two men shook hands. The pastor's grip was firm but cold.

"Be seated, sir," said Grimes. "May I offer you refreshment? Coffee? Tea? Or . . . ?"

"Tea, captain. Not strong. No milk. No sugar."

Grimes telephoned the pantry and made the order. He sat back in his chair, filled and lit his pipe.

The pastor said, "Do not smoke."

Grimes said, "This is my ship, sir. I make the rules."

"This may be your ship, Captain, but you neither own nor command this planet. And, as I understand it, you will be unable to lift from this world unless you are vouchsafed cooperation by myself and the elders of my church."

Grimes made a major production of sighing. Until he knew which way the wind was blowing or likely to blow he would have to do as bid. He put his pipe down in the ashtray.

Shirl came in, carrying a tray which she set on the coffee table. (Melinda Clay, in her capacity as purser, would still be dealing with the port officials.) In her very short uniform shorts she looked all legs.

Coffin looked at her disapprovingly then said, "Are all your female officers so indecently attired, Captain?"

Grimes said, "My female officers wear what is standard uniform for both the Federation Survey Service and the Merchant Service."

"Aboard the ships of Able Enterprises," said Coffin, "females are always decently covered."

And Drongo Kane, thought Grimes, would put his people in sackcloth and ashes as the rig of the day rather than lose a profitable trade. *And so would I*, he realized with some surprise.

Shirl glared at Coffin and strode out of the day cabin. Grimes poured the tea, which was far too weak for his taste, added milk and sugar to his own.

"I understand, Captain," said the pastor, "that you have various mechanical troubles. We on Salem, freed from the tyranny of the machine, are not so afflicted."

"It was machines, starships, that brought your ancestors here, sir."

"At times the Lord uses the Devil's tools. But His people should avoid doing so. Now, what are your requirements? What must you do to make your vessel spaceworthy?"

"I have to repair a bulkhead—just a matter of patching. I hope that a suitable plate will be available here. The shaft of my inertial drive governor must be renewed. My Mannschenn Drive has to be recalibrated. I understand that there is a workshop here, and a stock of spares and materials."

"Your understanding is correct, Captain. The workshop and the stores are the property of Able Enterprises. I am empowered to act as their agent."

"Any skilled labor, pastor?"

"We have blacksmiths, Captain, but nobody capable of carrying out the type of work that you seem to require."

"No matter. My own engineers can start earning their pay for a change." Grimes picked up his pipe, thought better of it and put it down again. "There's another matter, pastor. I don't need to tell you that a deviation, such as this one that I have been obliged to make, costs money. I am not loaded to capacity. Would there be any chance of a cargo of silkie hides to New Otago?"

"It is only wealthy worlds, such as El Dorado, that can afford such luxury clothing," said the pastor. "From what I have heard of New Otago I gain the impression that nobody there is either very rich or very poor."

"Perhaps," said Grimes hopefully, "there might be the possibility, some time in the not too distant future, of a shipment of hides from here to some market, somewhere. . . ."

"Able Enterprises," Coffin told him, "have the monopoly on the trade from Salem to Earth as well as to El Dorado. But you are a widely traveled man, Captain. You have your contacts throughout the Galaxy . . ." And did Grimes detect the gleam of cupidity in the pastor's eyes? "Perhaps, in your voyagings, you will be able to find other markets for our export. In such a case I am sure that some mutually profitable arrangement could be made."

Melinda Clay came in with various documents to be signed. Coffin looked at her even more disapprovingly than he had Shirl but said nothing until she had left.

He said, "So you employ the children of Ham aboard your vessel. But, from them, an indecent display of flesh is, I suppose, to be expected."

"Mphm," grunted Grimes.

Coffin got to his feet. "Almost I was tempted to forbid shore leave to yourself and your officers. But I realize that if there are, in the future, to be business dealings between you and ourselves there must be some familiarization. Your people must understand the nature of the cargo that they will be carrying. Too, it is not impossible that they, or at least some of them, will find the true Light. . . ." He drew himself to his full, not inconsiderable height. "But I strongly advise you, Captain, to see to it that your females are properly attired when they set foot on our soil. Otherwise I shall not be responsible for the consequences."

Probably, thought Grimes contemptuously, *your men would fly into a screaming tizzy at the sight of a woman's ankle.*

He said, "I'll see to it, pastor, that my people comport themselves properly."

"Do so, Captain. Tomorrow morning I shall have the spaceport workshop unlocked and shall be waiting for you there so that you and your engineers can tell me what you want."

"At about 0900?" asked Grimes.

"At seven of the clock," stated Coffin. "We, on this world do not waste the daylight hours that God sends us."

Grimes sent for his senior officers, received from them more detailed damage reports than the earlier ones, told them of his talk with Coffin. He said, "There will be shore leave. But you must make it plain to your people, the girls especially, that they are to avoid giving offense in any way. This is a very puritanical planet, so the ladies are to wear long skirts at all times. It will be as well, too, if there is no smoking in public."

Steerforth laughed. "That's going to hurt you, Captain."

"Too right it is," agreed Grimes. "But I suppose that I must set a good example for the rest of you." He turned to Florence Scott. "I'm afraid that it's an early rise and an early breakfast for you tomorrow morning, Flo. The pastor—he's the local boss cocky—is letting us use the Able Enterprises repair and maintenance facilities. I suggested that we meet him in the workshop at 0900 but he made it plain that, as far as he's concerned, the day's work starts at 0700. We have to play along.

"You can make contact with the local ship chandler, Melinda," he said to the catering officer, "and order any consumable stores necessary. Just try to remember that *Sister Sue* is not the flagship of Trans-Galactic Clippers! Oh, and if there are any locals aboard don't forget to keep Seiko out of sight . . ."

She grinned whitely and said, "I've read that article in *Star Scandals*, Captain. If any of these superstitious bastards got the idea that she's my familiar I might get barbecued."

"And Seiko almost certainly would be. And how are things in the time-twisting department, Dan?"

"All that are required are patience and a few pairs of steady hands," said the Mannschenn Drive engineer. "We shall have things re-assembled before Flo's pusher is ready."

"And then you'll make a balls of the recalibration," Ms Scott said. "It's happened before, you know."

"And that seems to be it," said Grimes. "A nightcap before you go?"

They accepted. When they finally left, Grimes overheard a scrap of conversation from the alleyway outside his door, Florence Scott talking to Daniel Grey.

"The old bastard's taking things remarkably well. I thought that he'd be having my guts for a necktie."

"He's insured," said Grey.

And I'll be surprised, thought Grimes, *if Lloyd's don't up my premiums.*

Chapter 17

The next morning Grimes, with Steerforth, Florence Scott and Juanita Garcia, partook of an early breakfast. The meal finished, the four of them made their way out of the ship, down the ramp to the scarred concrete of the apron, still wet from overnight showers. The sun was only just up, in a partly cloudy sky, and the air was decidedly chilly. The spaceport administration buildings toward which they were walking reminded Grimes of pictures that he had seen in his father's library, of small seaports on the Pacific coast of North America during the nineteenth century old style. There were the rather ramshackle wooden structures, the tallest of which was the control tower from which, incongruously, sprouted the antennae and scanners of modern communication and locating equipment. But there should have been a quay, thought Grimes, with square-rigged sailing vessels, whalers, alongside to complete the picture.

"Are you sure that we didn't, somehow, travel back in time, Captain?" asked Juanita. "It's not only the way that this place looks but the way that it smells, even. . . ."

Grimes removed his pipe from his mouth, exhaled the fumes of burning tobacco, waited until his sense of smell was again operational and then sniffed the air. Drifting down the light wind from the nearby town was the pleasant acridity of wood smoke from morning cooking fires.

He said to the second engineer, "In a way we have traveled back in time, Juanita. The colonists here deliberately put the clock back. Oh, well, it's their world and they're welcome to it."

There were signs of life around the administration buildings. As the party from the ship approached these a tall, black-clad figure emerged from one of the sheds, strode up to them. It was Pastor Coffin. He pulled a huge, silver watch from his waistcoat pocket, glared at it. He said, "You are late, Captain. It is already two minutes past the hour."

Grimes apologized, with a certain look of sincerity, saying that he had underestimated the time that it would take to walk from the ship. The pastor said coldly, "You spacemen . . ." He looked coldly at Juanita who, even in her white overalls, was indubitably feminine. "You spacepersons, with your machines waiting on you hand and foot, do not take enough healthy exercise. But come."

He led the way into the long shed from which he had emerged. The interior was gloomy. The windows were small and the few electric lights that had been switched on seemed to be doing their best to imitate oil lamps. What was their power source? wondered Grimes. Batteries, probably. In one corner was what was obviously a generator, which was not running. It, like the other machinery and equipment in the shed, would be the property of Able Enterprises.

"Can't we have some proper light?" asked Ms. Scott irritably. "I see a jenny there that's doing nothing for its living."

"You may start the machine," said Coffin to Grimes. "But you will be charged for its hire."

"We must have proper illumination," said Grimes. "Flo, can you get that thing going?"

"No trouble, Captain. I cut my teeth on diesels."

She walked to the generator, inspected it, cracked fuel valves and switched on the electric starter. The thing coughed briefly and then settled down to a steady beat. Juanita found other light switches and, within seconds, the interior of the workshop was bathed by the harsh glow of the overhead fluorescents.

Steerforth said to Grimes, as he looked around,

"Drongo Kane could almost build a ship from scratch with the stuff that he's got stashed in here."

"As long as there's some suitable plating . . ." said Grimes.

"And we shall probably have to use that lathe," put in Ms. Scott. "To turn down a new shaft for the governor."

"I rely upon you," said Coffin, "to maintain a strict tally of all materials utilized and of all machinery employed."

"You can start the timekeeping now, Mr. Steerforth," Grimes ordered his chief officer. "When I go back to the ship I shall arrange for you to be relieved by Mr. Kershaw."

Steerforth pulled a notebook from his pocket and made entries.

Coffin accompanied Grimes back to *Little Sister*.

He said, "Perhaps you think it strange, Captain, that I should allow your people free run of the workshop."

Grimes said, "Frankly yes, pastor. I expected that you or one of your people would remain to keep an eye on things."

The pastor made a sound that approximated a chuckle. "We do business with Able Enterprises but we do not have to like them, any more than we have to like you. In the final analysis, it matters not if one party of unbelievers, as repre-

sented by yourself, robs another party of unbelievers. But I think that you are, according to
your lights, dim though they be, an honorable
man ..."

"Thank you," said Grimes dryly.

"And, of course, the port dues and such that
you will pay will hasten the day when our project shall be completed ..."

Project? wondered Grimes. Oh, yes. The Ark
that would survive the eventual collapse of the
Universe.

He asked, "Has work on the project actually
commenced yet?"

"We have commissioned research," the pastor
told him. "The salvation vessel will not, of course,
be mechanically propelled. It will be a sailing
ship of Space."

"Mphm," grunted Grimes.

They had reached the foot of the gangway. Not
very enthusiastically Grimes invited Coffin aboard
the ship for morning tea. He was relieved when
the pastor declined the invitation, saying that he
was a busy man. He went aboard himself, sent for
the second officer and told him to take over from
Mr. Steerforth in the workshop. He discussed various matters with the chief MD engineer and the
catering officer. Then he sent for Shirl and Darleen,
looked them up and down and ordered them to
change into less revealing uniforms, telling them
that they were to accompany him on a stroll to

the town, which was also the seaport. He waited for them in the after airlock. When they joined him they were dressed in concealing (more or less) white overalls, standard working rig.

The day was warming up now although there was still a nip in the breeze. The road from the spaceport to the seaport was little more than a rough track and the walk was rather more arduous than Grimes had anticipated. Still, he enjoyed it, looking with interest at the vegetation on either side of the path. He was no botanist and could see little difference between these trees and Terran pines, between these bushes and gorse and broom. Perhaps the flora was of Terran origin and had been introduced by the colonists. Perhaps not. It did not much matter. It was the indigenous fauna with which he was concerned.

Shirl complained, "Why must we wear these things, John? We want to run, to feel the sun and the fresh air on our bodies."

He told her, "You know why. You've read your pal Fenella's story about what happened when she was here."

"Yes," said Darleen. "But Fenella's toys were not only undressed. They were . . ."

"And perhaps we could," suggested Shirl.

"Not here, not now," said Grimes hastily; nonetheless he did think that a nearby clump of broom would provide adequate cover.

They came to the town. There were wooden

houses, none of more than one story, except for
the church, with its little bell tower. Lace curtains covered the small windows but Grimes
thought that some of these were drawn aside for a
surreptitious peep as the three strangers made
their way down the narrow street. But there were
very few people abroad and the occasional black-
clad man or woman whom they encountered
scowled at them suspiciously.

Suddenly Shirl and Darleen, walking to either
side of Grimes, fell silent. This, for them, was
most unusual. He looked at first one and then the
other. Their faces were pale, frightened almost.

He asked, "What's wrong?"

"Don't you . . . smell it, John?" said Darleen.

"Smell what?" he demanded.

There was the salty tang of the nearby sea and
with it, not unpleasant, a hint of decaying seaweed.
And there was the acridity of tar and, from a
baker's shop, the mouth-watering aroma of freshly
baked bread.

"The . . . The smell of fear," whispered Shirl.
"And of pain . . . And of helplessness . . ."

And something was happening on the waterfront. Suddenly there was a growing clamor, the
sound of many voices, shouting exultantly. There
was singing; it sounded like a hymn of some
kind. And now and again there was a thin, high,
unhuman screaming.

Grimes quickened his pace and the girls kept

step, hurrying through the narrow, winding dirt street. They emerged on to a wide quay, from which protruded finger jetties. At two of these, large schooners were already alongside; other schooners, four of them, were coming in from seaward, running free, their shabby sails widespread to catch the last of the dying breeze. The jetties were crowded with the singing, shouting, black-clad people, although those at which the ships had yet to come alongside were less congested.

To one of these Grimes, followed by Shirl and Darleen, made his way. He clambered up on to one of the ox-drawn wagons that was waiting there so that he could see over the heads of the crowd, watch what was happening. The girls followed him. The driver of this vehicle, a burly, black-bearded giant, turned in his seat to stare at them.

He growled, "Get off, you!" Then, as he saw the uniforms, his manner changed. "Oh, you're spacers, aren't you? Off that ship. You can stay, but only until I pick up my load."

"What will your load be?" asked Grimes.

"The harvest of the sea, spacer. Looks as though the boats have done well this trip. They're low in the water."

Yes, thought Grimes, looking at the approaching schooner. *She's down to her marks, or over them . . .*

The triangular sails were coming down now and being lashed smartly to the booms. That skipper, thought Grimes, knew his job. With only a ballooning jib to provide steerage way, the ship ghosted in, drifted gently alongside the jetty. Lines were thrown, caught by men on the quay, their eyes slipped over bollards. The jib came down with a run.

The hatches, one abaft the foremast, the other abaft the mainmast, were already open. From his vantage point Grimes could see into both of these. In the main hold were bloody pelts—black and brown and gray and golden. In the fore hold was living cargo, a squirming mass in which the same colors predominated. And it was from this hold that the thin, high screaming came.

And there was a faint scream from either Shirl or Darleen.

Grimes said to the driver, making a statement rather than asking a question, "Silkies . . ."

"What else, spacer."

"But those live ones. In the forward hold . . ."

"Pups o' course."

Grimes, shipowner and shipmaster, was becoming interested and for more than humanitarian reasons. "It seems to me," he said, "that the adult silkies were skinned where they were slaughtered. But why were the pups taken alive? If they'd been killed and skinned too, so much more cargo could have been carried."

The driver laughed condescendingly.

"It's easy to see that you are not on the fur trade, spacer. The people from the Able ships know how we do things. The pelts of the pups are much finer than those of the adults. It has been found that if they are carried for days in a ship's hold, even well salted down, they go rotten. So the pup pelts are brought in still on the pups. And then the pups are skinned in the factories."

"But I would think," said Grimes, "that the pups themselves would die and go rotten, and their skins around them, during a voyage in those conditions."

"Not them. They're not like us. They're hardy beasts. Oh, those on the bottom will be near dead by the time that they're discharged—but they'll all soon be dead in any case."

There was a slight shift of wind. Over the wagon drifted the reek of stale blood, of corruption and of excrement. *Money stinks*, thought Grimes sourly, choking down his rising nausea.

But he decided to stay for a while. The booms of the schooner were being used as swinging derricks. In the holds the longshoremen were making up slings of the bloody pelts, throwing the squirming pups into cargo nets, others were in gangs manning the tackles. Two wagons had drawn up alongside the ship to receive cargo.

"I'm next in line," said the driver. "You'd better get off 'less you want to ride back among a load o' pups."

"I think we'll walk," said Grimes. "But thanks all the same. And thank you for the information."

Shirl and Darleen jumped down to the wharf decking. Grimes followed.

"Let us get out of here!" said the girls as one.

Chapter 18

They walked slowly back to the ship, at first in silence.

"Humans are very cruel . . ." said Shirl at last.

"We have studied your history," said Darleen.

"So?" said Grimes.

"So all through your history," went on Darleen, "you have slaughtered, for your own profit, not only beings lacking real intelligence but those who are as intelligent as you, although in a different way. The whales, the dolphins . . ."

"We have seen the error of our ways," said Grimes. "We are trying to put things right."

"We? Do you speak for all of your race, John? Oh, you were sent to this world by the Old Crocodile to try to save the silkies—but there is money in this stinking fur trade, just as there has been money in other trades in which Drongo Kane has been involved. Women and boys from their primitive worlds to the brothels of New Venusberg, for example. And Kane is not alone. There are many like him, to whom the only god, among all the odd gods, is money. At times we have suspected that even you worship this god."

"Don't drag religion into it," snapped Grimes. Then, "You've seen silkies now. Are they intelligent beings?"

Shirl laughed bitterly.

"We saw," she said, "a squirming mass of very young beings, wallowing in their own filth, terrified, speechless. Imagine that you are a non-human being from some other planet, seeing human babies in a similar state. Would you think that they were intelligent beings?"

"So you are not sure," said Grimes.

"We are not sure. We know that the fur trade is a brutal one, that is all. We shall have to meet adult silkies and talk with them . . ."

"Talk with them?"

"As we talked with the kangaroos, back on Earth. Oh, they are not truly intelligent but they are capable of evolving, doing over a very long time what our ancestors did, with outside help, in a very short time."

"The crimes of genetic engineers are many," said Grimes.

"We resent that," they said in chorus.

"I was speaking in jest. And, in any case, the pair of you are much better looking than a silky in any age group."

"We should hope so. But what would a silky think of us? Horribly ugly brutes who slaughter and torture."

"They must learn," said Grimes, "that all human beings—and that includes you, after all you are officially human—are not the same."

"Then we shall have to meet them," said Shirl. "We shall have to commune with them."

They passed through the town and then made a detour, following one of the wagons, with its load of shrieking pups, that had made its way inland from the waterfront. It was headed toward a long shed, came to a halt outside its open door. Men clambering up on to the vehicle, threw to the ground the small, squirming, furry bodies. Other men dragged these inside the building.

"We ... We would rather not see what is happening," said Shirl.

"Neither would I," said Grimes, "but I'm afraid that I have to."

It was an experience that would live long in his memory. The pups, hanging by hooks from a sort of primitive overhead conveyor belt, were being flayed alive and their still-living bodies thrown into a steaming cauldron while their pelts, treated with far greater respect, were neatly stacked on tables.

A burly man, a foreman, bloody knife in hand, approached Grimes.

"What are you doing here, spacer?" he demanded.

"Just ... Just looking." And then, unable to restrain his disgust, "Is that necessary?"

"Is what necessary?"

"Couldn't you kill the pups before you skin them?"

"Keep your nose out of things about which you know nothing. Kill them first, and ruin the pelts? Everybody knows that a pup has to be skinned while it's still living."

"But ... It's cruel."

"Cruel? How so, spacer? Everybody knows, surely, that the Lord God gave Man authority over all lesser beings. How can the exercise of divinely granted authority be cruel?"

"It need not be."

"It does need to be, spacer, if the high quality pelts are not to be ruined. Too, is not God Himself often cruel in the light of our limited understanding?"

With an effort, Grimes restrained himself from saying, *Thank God I'm an agnostic.*

"But I have work to do, spacer. And you will have seen that no effort is spared to ensure that the pelts we export are of high quality. The pastor

has told us that you may be interested in entering
the trade."

Grimes made his retreat to the fresh, open air
but was delayed as a fresh batch of feebly struggling, almost inaudibly whining pups was dragged
into the slaughterhouse. When he got outside he
walked unsteadily to where Shirl and Darleen
were waiting for him.

He muttered, as much to himself as to them,
"This filthy trade must be stopped!"

When they got back to the spaceport, to the ship,
his nausea was almost gone. He saw two women
taking a gentle stroll around the ship. One was in
uniform, but with slacks instead of the usual very
short skirt, the other was wearing what looked
like a modified version of the traditional kimono.
But who was that with her, in uniform? It was
neither the radio officer nor the catering officer;
her face was not black. It was none of the female
engineer officers.

The two women saw Grimes, walked to meet
him.

"Captain-san," said Tomoko, bowing.

But it was Tomoko who was wearing the uniform.

"Captain-san," said the other, also bowing.

Her glossy black hair was piled high on her
head. Her face was very pale, white, almost, and
her lips an unnatural scarlet. Rather incongru-

ously she was wearing a pair of huge dark spectacles.

"Who is this . . . geisha?" demanded Grimes of Tomoko.

But he knew. He had recognized, although with some incredulity, the voice.

"Captain-san," said the third officer, "Seiko-san wanted some exercise, some fresh air . . ."

"She needs neither," said Grimes.

"And you had made it plain," went on Tomoko, "that she was not to appear before any of the colonists in her true form, as a robot. But I have cosmetics, and a wig, and suitable clothing for her. Her eyes, of course, must remain hidden . . ."

"And her body," said Grimes.

"Oh, no, Captain-san. I have painted her all over, from her head to her feet, with the right touches of color . . ."

Grimes laughed. "That was unnecessary. A naked female body would give even more affront to the people here than would a robot. All right, Tomoko. And Seiko. Carry on with your stroll. But don't stray too far from the ship."

As he mounted the gangway he muttered, "Exercise . . . Fresh air . . . Why not sunshine while she was about it?"

"She's only human . . ." said Shirl or Darleen.

Chapter 19

Grimes, with Shirl and Darleen as company, had a sandwich lunch in his quarters. Steerforth came up to join his captain and the two girls for coffee and a talk. Grimes told his chief officer what he had seen.

"Whether or not the silkies are intelligent," he concluded, "this fur trade is a sickening business. The slaughter of the pups especially."

"Salem is a long way from Earth, sir," said Steerforth. "And there's big money involved, and the El Dorado Corporation has a finger in this particular pie. I need hardly tell you, captain, how many Gs the EDC can pile on when its interests are threatened."

"Mphm. And meanwhile, back at the ranch,"

asked Grimes, "how have things been going?"

Steerforth laughed. "I wandered over to the workshop just after I'd had my lunch, to relieve Kershaw for his. Flo and her gang were having their troubles. She was stomping up and down with a sandwich in one hand and a spanner in the other—she told me that they couldn't spare the time to return to the ship for a proper meal— and bawling out Calamity Cassie, who'd just perpetrated some piece of spectacular clumsiness, and calling down curses on Able Enterprises. . . ."

"Why Able Enterprises?" asked Grimes.

"To quote Flo," said Steerforth, " 'This isn't a workshop. It's a fornicating junk shop!' Even I—and I'm no engineer—could see her point. That machinery—the generator, the turret lathe and so on—must have been bought on the cheap from Noah's Ark after she became a total loss on Mount Ararat."

Grimes laughed. "Drongo Kane's an astute businessman. He's not going to leave new, highly expensive equipment unattended on a world like this. There are just the essentials here, and no more. His own engineers would be expected to make do with what's in the workshop. My engineers'll just have to do the same. Did Flo come up with any estimation of the time it'll take her to complete the repairs?"

"That she did not, sir. I got snarled at for daring to ask. 'First of all,' she yelled, 'I have to repair the machines that I shall have to use to repair my own machinery!' Of course, she should never have allowed Cassie within spitting distance of that lathe.''

"Spread it around," said Grimes, "that I'm in a vile bad temper, like a raging lion seeking whom I might devour, especially if it happens to be one, any one, of my engineers. This is all costing me money." He laughed rather humorlessly. "And if Admiral Damien doesn't see me compensated I *shall* be in a bad temper!

"Meanwhile you might get one of the lifeboats ready for an atmospheric flight. I'd like to take it out for a run tomorrow morning."

"The boats are always ready, sir," said Steerforth stiffly. Then, "Which officers are you taking with you?"

"Just Shirl and Darleen," Grimes told him. "It's all part of their training."

"Can't Seiko come with us, John?" asked Shirl. "She'll enjoy the trip."

"*Seiko?*" Grimes considered the idea then repeated, less dubiously, "Seiko?"

"Why not, sir?" said Steerforth. "I mean no offense, but you do, at times, display a certain aptitude for getting into trouble. And," he added hastily, "for getting out of it. But now and again you've needed help. Shirl and Darleen, with their somewhat unorthodox martial skills, will be quite good bodyguards. And so would be Seiko. She's intelligent. And she's strong. You know those absurdly heavy lids on the yeast culture vats, how it always takes at least two people to lift one off? The other day I saw Seiko lift one by herself, using one hand only. And, even more important, she's loyal to you. It's gotten to the stage where nobody dare say anything unkind about you in her hearing."

"Mphm . . ." Grimes filled and lit his pipe. "But there's still the attitude of the colonists toward robots to be considered. We might find ourselves in some situation where Seiko's presence would be like a red rag to a bull."

"But nobody would know that she is a robot, sir. I was with Tomoko when she applied the make-up, the body paint, the cosmetics. And Tomoko made a very thorough job, even to a merkin. You could strip her and nobody would dream that she wasn't a human woman—as long as you left her dark glasses on."

"All right. I'll take Seiko along. With her and Shirl and Darleen I could fight off an army."

"And Cassie, to look after the lifeboat's engine?" asked Steerforth.

"That would be tempting Providence," said Grimes.

The next morning, right after breakfast, Grimes, with Shirl, Darleen and Seiko, made their way to the Number 1 boat bay. Steerforth was already there, making a last-minute check. With him was Florence Scott, grumbling audibly that she had more important things to occupy her time than getting things ready for the Old Man's joy ride. Seiko, clad not in kimono but working rig like that worn by Shirl and Darleen, was carrying two large hampers of food for the biologically human members of the party. Her rather too elaborately coiled glossy black wig looked odd over the white boiler suit. *An aristocratic Japanese lady,* thought Grimes, *dressed to make a tour of inspection of a sewage conversion plant . . .*

"She's all yours, Captain," said Steerforth, emerging from the boat's airlock.

"The innie's OK," said Ms. Scott. She grinned sourly. "Just as well that I never let Calamity Cassie overhaul it."

"Thank you," said Grimes. "I'll leave matters in your capable hands, gentlefolk. Expect me back late afternoon or early evening."

"Cleo will be maintaining a listening watch," said Steerforth. "Just in case. If you should get into trouble it'd be no use calling the so-called Aerospace Control. Their operators never seem to be on duty."

"And never on Sunday," said Grimes. "And today's Sunday. Oh, by the way, Flo, if the pastor or any of his minions show up to complain about your breaking the Sabbath in the workshop, don't try to argue. Just look pious and knock off."

"You're the captain," she said. "And the owner."

Grimes followed the women into the boat, went forward to the control cab, sat in the pilot's seat. He operated the switch that would close the airlock doors, the other one that caused the securing clamps to fall away. He spoke into his microphone, "Number 1 boat to control room. Ready to self-eject."

"Eject at will, Number 1," came the reply.

Grimes operated the boat bay door from the control cab, although this could have been done from the ship's control room. Through the forward window he saw the double valve opening and beyond the outward swinging metal plates blue sky and fluffy white clouds. The miniature inertial drive unit grumbled to itself and the boat lifted a few centimeters clear of the deck and then, obedient to Grimes' touch, slid forward and out.

Had his ship been berthed at a normal spaceport Grimes would now have reported his movements to Aerospace Control and would, in fact, have obtained prior permission to hold a boat drill from the Port Captain. But here there was no Port Captain. For much of the time there was not even a Communications Officer. (But there would surely be, thought Grimes, some official seeing to it that port dues and other charges were paid by visiting ships.)

Grimes circled *Sister Sue* at control-room altitude. He saw Tomoko and Cleo Jones standing by the big viewports. They waved to him. He waved back. Still circling, he lifted steadily. The seaport was now in view, with the jetties and, alongside them, the big schooners. From this height the blue-gray ocean looked calm. To the northeast was a large island with three peaks, one tall and two little more than hummocks. To the north was a chain of islets. Below the surface of the sea were brown blotches that could either be rocks or beds of some kelp-like weed. Grimes wished that he had maps and charts to cover this planet. He would have to make his own. In fact he was starting to do just that; the boat was fitted with a Survey Service surplus datalog, not at all standard equipment for small craft carried by merchant starships.

He set course for the archipelago, reducing altitude as he made his approach. Using binoculars he could make out marine creatures swimming below the surface of the sea. Silkies? Could be. Behind him he heard Shirl, Darleen and Seiko chattering, pointing things out to each other. He tried to ignore them.

Then, "Look!" he heard Shirleen exclaim. "That rock! It must be a sikly colony!"

He realized that she was talking to him, swung

his glasses in the direction that she had indicated. The surface of the small, rocky island seemed to be alive—but there was not the display of gloriously colored pelts that he would have expected. There was just a slowly heaving olive-green carpet. There was something there, something alive, but it could be no more than some form of motile plant life.

He said, "The silkies' hides aren't that color."

"There are silkies there," stated Darleen firmly. "We can . . . *feel* it."

"Oh, all right," said Grimes. "It costs nothing to have a closer look."

The boat dropped steadily, its mini-innie hammering noisily. Suddenly there was a flurry of motion on the islet. That olive-green carpet went into a frenzy, seemed to be tearing itself to pieces, rags of it flying into the air, falling into the sea. And the silkies who had been hidden under the broad, fleshy leaves of seaweed slithered rapidly into the water, a spectacular eruption of black and brown and golden and silver bodies, the pups first, being pushed and rolled off the rock by their parents, the adults last of all.

(The silky-hunters' schooners, thought Grimes, would be making a silent approach, not a noisy one as he was. And probably the masthead lookouts would not be deceived, not every time, by the silkies' camouflage.)

"Are you landing, John?" asked Shirl.

"What good will that do?" countered Grimes.

"Once you have shut off that noisy thing—" Darleen gestured toward the engine casing "—we may be able to call the silkies back."

"I suppose it's worth trying," said Grimes.

He made his final approach with great caution. The surface of the rock seemed to be uniformly flat, although in parts was still covered with small heaps of the weed. Grimes did his best to avoid these; they might well conceal rocky upthrustings or crevasses. Finally the belly skids made contact and the shock absorbers sighed gently and the inertial drive unit subsided into silence.

"We're here," said Grimes unnecessarily. He raised the ship on the NST radio but, although he could have reported the boat's exact location as read from the datalog, did not do so. It suddenly occurred to him that the pastor, having learned that Grimes was on a snooping expedition, might be maintaining a listening watch of his own.

"But where are you, sir?" demanded Steerforth irritably.

"Oh, just on some bloody island. I thought that it would be a good place for a swim, and then lunch."

With that the chief officer would have to be content. But surely he would have tracked the boat on the ship's radar and would have a very good idea as to where she was. But what of Aerospace Control? Had some technician broken the

Sabbath to get their radar working? Grimes was certain, however, that those antennae on the control tower had not been rotating while that structure was still within sight of the boat.

He opened the airlock doors and then led the way out into the open air.

Chapter 20

There was no wind and the piles of decomposing seaweed were steaming in the sun, as were the deposits of ordure. The mixed aroma, although strong, was not altogether unpleasant. The silkies, decided Grimes, must be vegetarians. He and the three women walked around the little island, being careful where they put their feet. The shape of this flat rock was roughly rectangular, one kilometer by five hundred meters. On the northern face were low cliffs, about ten meters above sea level. On the southern side there was a gradual slope right into the water, a natural ramp by which the silkies could gain access to their rookery.

Grimes said, "It's a pity that we scared them all off."

"What else did you expect?" demanded Shirl. "They must have thought that the boat was something new being used by the fur hunters."

"But we can try to call them back," said Darleen.

She kicked off her shoes, shrugged out of her boiler suit, stepped out of her brief underwear. She waded out into the still water. "It's *cold!*" she complained. But she walked on, slowly but steadily. Grimes wondered why she did not swim. Then suddenly she assumed a squatting posture, lowering herself until she was completely submerged. She lost her balance of course and floated, face down, her prominent buttocks well above the surface. From around the region of her head came a flurry of bubbles.

She came up for air, inhaling deeply, and then repeated her original maneuver. Again she came up for air and this time struck out for the shore. She waded out to where Grimes, with Shirl and Seiko, was standing.

"It is no use," she said. "I cannot sing under the water."

"I can," said Seiko. "I am guaranteed to be waterproof at any depth. But what must I sing?"

"It will be a call," Darleen told her. "A sound that will carry a long way, a very long way, under the sea. When we were on Earth we studied many things. We listened to the recordings of the whale songs and tried to understand them and to make the same sort of music ourselves. And it was a whale song that I was trying to sing just now. Its meaning is, put into words, 'Come to me. Come to me.' "

"I suppose that it was Admiral Damien who suggested this course of studies," commented Grimes.

"It was," Darleen admitted. "But he never thought to have taught us to sing under the water."

"What sounds must I make?" asked Seiko.

Darleen started to sing. It was an eerie ululation with an odd rhythm. It was something that one felt rather than merely listened to. There was the impression of loneliness, of hunger for close contact. It was a call, a call that any sentient being, on hearing it, would be bound to answer.

And the call was being answered.

From nowhere, it seemed, the birds—if they were birds—were coming in, squawking discordantly, circling overhead. Grimes didn't like the looks of them—those long, curved, vicious beaks, those wings that looked leathery rather than feathery, those whiplike, spiked tails ... But Darleen sang on, and was joined by Seiko.

And those blasted flying things were getting lower all the time.

Shirl tore a piece of seaweed from a nearby pile, a broad, fleshy slab. She threw it, spinning lopsidedly, aloft. It hit one of the birds. It staggered off course, splashed clumsily into the sea. It seemed to be injured, fluttering and croaking.

At once the entire overhead flock ceased their circling and dived on to their disabled companion in a feeding frenzy. It was not a pretty sight. By the time they had finished, at least half a dozen stripped carcasses were sinking to the bottom and the wings of several more of the creatures did not seem to be in good enough repair to carry them for any great distance.

Darleen stopped singing, although Seiko continued. The New Alician followed Shirl's example and armed herself with a makeshift throwing weapon. The birds, their grisly feast (or the first course of it) over, took to the air again and this time made straight for Grimes and his party. Shirl and Darleen effectively launched their missiles, and again, and again, but this time the predators ignored their fallen companions.

"Stop singing!" barked Grimes to Seiko.

Enchanted by the sound of her own voice she ignored him.

"Stop singing!" Who the hell did she think she was? Madam Butterfly? "Stop singing!"

With his right index finger he made a jab for where he estimated her navel, with its ON/OFF switch, to be under the concealing clothing. It hurt him more than it did her but he did succeed in gaining her attention.

She turned to him and said severely, "That was not necessary, captain."

"It most certainly was, you . . . you animated cuckoo clock!"

"If you say so."

But the flying things had lost interest. They circled the party from the boat one last time and then flapped off to the eastward. One of them, a straggler, voided its bowels. It seemed that it must have made allowance for deflection; the noisome mess came down with a splatter on to Grimes' right shoulder, befouling his gold-braided shoulder-board.

"Don't you have a superstition," asked Shirl sweetly, "that that is a sign of good luck?"

Grimes snarled wordlessly and went back into the boat to find some tissues to clean himself off.

When he rejoined the others Seiko was getting ready to make her submarine solo. She had taken off her clothing and was standing there beside the naked Darleen, in her skillfully applied coat of paint looking far more human than the flesh-and-blood girl; there was no oddness about the joints of her lower limbs, no exaggerated heaviness of the haunches. Tomoko had certainly done a good job on her, even to the coral nipples and the black pubic hair.

The robot removed her dark glasses, handed them to Shirl. Now, with those utterly colorless eyes behind which there was a hint of movement, she did look unhuman—but she was still beautiful.

She said, "It is a pity that I cannot take off the wig, but it is secured by adhesive. . . ."

Grimes wondered what that beautifully elaborate coiffeur would look like when she came out of the water.

She walked down to the verge of the calm sea, Darleen beside her. Her movements were more graceful than those of the New Alician—more graceful but less natural. She waded out, Darleen waded out. Darleen stopped when the water was at shoulder level. Seiko, with her much greater specific gravity, went on going. Before long she had completely vanished.

Had she started to sing yet?

Grimes supposed that she had done so.

He hoped that it would be the silkies who answered the call and not, as on the first trial, some totally unexpected and unpleasant predators. He looked out over the sea, to the weed patches, to the low, dark shapes of the other rocky islets. He saw no signs of life.

Suddenly Darleen called out something. He could not make out the words. He saw her dive from her standing posture, her lower legs and long feet briefly visible above the surface. By his side Shirl hastily stripped then ran out into the sea and also dived from view.

Should he join them?

This would be foolish, especially as he did not know what was happening. Besides, he was not all that good a swimmer. All that he could do was wait.

At last a head reappeared above the surface, then another. Shirl and Darleen swam slowly in until the water was shallow enough for them to find footing, then waded the rest of the way. Grimes went down to meet them.

"What's happening?" he demanded.

"Seiko . . ." gasped Darleen.

"We . . . We've lost Seiko . . ." added Shirl.

Darleen recovered her breath and told her story. She had watched Seiko walking along the smooth rock of the sea bottom, presumably singing as she did so. And then, quite suddenly, she had vanished. Darleen dived then and swam underwater to where she had last seen Seiko. There was a crevasse, not very wide but very, very deep. Shirl joined her and both of them tried to swim down into this fissure. They had glimpsed, in the depths, a pale glimmer that might have been Seiko's body—and then even that had vanished.

"We shall miss her," said Shirl sadly.

Everybody aboard *Sister Sue* would miss her, thought Grimes. Robot she might be (might have been?) but she was a very real personality. Her father, who had played Pygmalion to her Galatea, would be saddened when he was told of Seiko's passing.

He said, "If we had deep diving equipment we might be able to do something. But we haven't . . ."

He looked out over the calm sea, to where he had last seen Seiko. He saw something break surface and momentarily felt a wild hope. But it was not the lost robot. It was a great, gleaming, golden shape and it was followed by others, golden, rich brown, black, silvery grey. The silkies, called by Seiko's song, were coming back.

"We have company," he said to the girls. "Get ready to talk."

Chapter 21

They retreated toward the center of the islet, making their stand by the boat. Shirl and Darleen did not resume their clothing although they had carried it with them, also the boiler suit, shoes and sunglasses that Seiko had been wearing.

"It will be better," said Darleen to Grimes, "if we meet the silkies naked. They will associate clothes with humans, the sort of humans who have been slaughtering them. Perhaps you, too, should undress . . ."

"Not bloody likely," said Grimes.

As a matter of fact he was already feeling naked. He should have brought some sort of weaponry from the ship, either a Minetti automatic pistol or a hand laser. Or both.

He watched the silkies lolloping up the natural ramp. Great, ugly—apart from their beautiful pelts—brutes they were, like obscenely obese Terran seals, more like fur-covered slugs than seals, perhaps, with hardly any distinction between heads and bodies, with tiny, gleaming eyes and wide, lipless mouths which they opened to emit not unmusical grunting sounds. And Shirl and Darleen were making similar noises, although it was more cooing than grunting.

Friends . . . The words somehow formed themselves in Grimes' mind. *Friends. We are friends. Friends.*

But the grunted reply held doubt, skepticism.

Shirl went on singing her song of peace and Darleen whispered to Grimes, "It might be better if you went back into the boat, John, to leave us to deal with these . . . people."

"No," said Grimes stubbornly. After all, he was the captain, wasn't he? And captains do not leave junior officers to face a danger while retiring to safety. And he already had Seiko's death (do robots die?) on his conscience.

Both the girls were singing again, in chorus. Perhaps, thought Grimes, he should join in—but he knew neither the tune nor the words. And the silkies, grunting, were still advancing. Belatedly Grimes realised that those on the wings of the oncoming column had accelerated their rate of advance, were executing a pincer movement. He turned, to see that his retreat to the boat was cut off.

Friends. . . . We come as friends. . . .

And were those wordless grunts making sense, or were the silkies pushing their message telepathically?

You . . . friends. Perhaps. Him—no. NO.

It was his clothing, thought Grimes. Perhaps the captains of Drongo Kane's ships had accompanied the fur hunters on their forays. Perhaps anybody wearing gold braid on his shoulders and on his cap was as much a murderer as the axe-, knife- and harpoon-wielding colonists in their rough working clothes.

Shirl and Darleen were getting the message. They closed in on Grimes, one on either side of him. They went on singing. And what was the burden of their song now; *Love me, love my dog . . . ?*

Whatever it was it made no difference.

Even on land the clumsy-seeming silkies could be amazingly quick when they wanted to be. A golden-furred giant reared up impossibly on its tail and hind flippers before Grimes and then fell upon him, knocking him sprawling. He heard the girls scream as they were similarly dealt with. And then there he was, on his back, a great, befurred and whiskered face over his. At least—

there are, more often than not, small, compensatory mercies—the thing's breath was quite sweet.

A flipper, a great slab of heavily muscled meat, lay heavily on his chest, making breathing difficult. Other flippers held his legs down and others, working clumsily but surely, were spreading wide his arms. He squirmed and managed to turn his head to the right. He saw that his right wrist, supported by a flipper that had closed around it like a limp mitten, had been raised from the ground. And he saw that a wide mouth, displaying the large, blunt teeth of the herbivore, was open, was about to close upon his hand. He remembered, in a flash, the horror stories he had heard about the silkies, their raids on coastwise villages, the mutilation of their victims. It made sense, a horrid sort of sense. It was only his hands, his tool-making, weapon-making, weapon-wielding hands that had given man dominion over the intelligent natives of this world.

He wondered if the silkies would kill him after they had chewed his hands off. It didn't much matter; he would very soon die of loss of blood.

The chorus of grunts all around him changed. There was the strong impression of fear, alarm. Had Steerforth, using the Number 2 boat, come to the rescue? But although there was noise enough the distinctive clatter of an inertial drive unit was absent.

A human arm came into his field of view, a hand caught the mutilation-intent silkie by the scruff of its almost nonexistent neck, lifted and made a sidewise fling in the same motion. A foot thudded into the side of the beast who was holding Grimes down. He caught confused glimpses of a naked female body in violent motion. At one stage four of the silkies succeeded, by sheer weight, in capturing her—Shirl? Darleen?—imprisoning her under the heaving mound of their bodies. But Shirl and Darleen were dancing around the outskirts of this living tumulus, kicking, burying their hands into soft fur and tugging ineffectually.

There was a sort of eruption and Seiko, the black hair of her once elaborate wig in wild disarray about her face, rose from its midst, stepping slowly and gracefully down over the struggling bodies. She walked to Grimes, caught him by the hands (and it was strange that her hands should be so cold, human-seeming as they were) and lifted him effortlessly to his feet.

She said, "I am sorry that I was late, Captain-san. But it was a long climb back up."

"You got here in time," Grimes told her. "And that's all that matters."

"The silkies . . ." said Shirl.

Yes, the silkies. They were retreating to the sea, but slowly.

Darleen ran after them, let herself be immersed

in that ebbing tide of multi-colored bodies. She
was singing again. Shirl joined her. Seiko stayed
with Grimes but she, too was singing.

Fantastically the tide turned. Led by Shirl and
Darleen the silkies came slowly back. The two
New Alicians draped themselves decoratively
about Grimes, their arms about his neck. Seiko
stood behind him, her hands on his shoulders.
And they sang, all three of them, and the silkies'
song in return held, at last, a note of acceptance.
One of the beasts—was it the golden-furred giant
who had knocked Grimes down?—made a slow,
somehow stately approach to the humans (the
true human, the two humans by courtesy, the
pseudo-human). He (Grimes assumed that it was
he) gently placed one huge flipper on the toe of
Grimes' right shoe.

"Touch his flipper with your hand, John," whispered Darleen.

Grimes, who kept himself reasonably fit, managed this without having to squat. He straightened.

"You are accepted," said Shirl.

"It makes a change," said Grimes, "from having
my hands eaten."

The musical conversation with the silkies continued. Becoming bored, Grimes pulled out and
filled his pipe.

"Stop!" Shirleen snapped. "To these people
fire is one of the badges of the murderer, just as
clothing is."

At last it was over. The silkies returned to the sea. Grimes and the girls went back into the boat. The clothing of Shirl, Darleen and Seiko had been lost in the scuffle but this, in this day and age, did not much matter. In the ship's sauna everybody was used to seeing everybody else naked.

Grimes set course back to the spaceport. For most of the flight Shirl and Darleen amused themselves by trying to restore Seiko's borrowed hair to some semblance of order. (That wig would never be the same again.) Grimes lent her his sunglasses.

He decided to land the boat by the after airlock rather than to bring her directly into the boat bay. Cleo Jones had informed him, when he called in to say that he was on the way back, that there was some slight trouble with the boat bay doors which had been discovered after his departure and which was still not rectified.

The belly skids made gentle contact with the dirty concrete of the apron. Grimes shut down the inertial drive, opened the airlock doors. The four of them stepped out into the pleasantly warm, late afternoon sunlight.

Grimes joked, "I hope that Mr. Steerforth doesn't give you girls a bawling out for being in incorrect uniform!"

But it was not only Steerforth who strode down the ramp from the ship's after airlock. Pastor Coffin,

in his severe black with its minimal white trim-
mings, was with him, was in the lead.

Coffin's craggy face was pale with fury. He glared
at the three naked women. He declaimed, "So
you have deigned to return from your orgy, your
debauching of these once innocent creatures. . . ."

"I wish that there had been an orgy . . ." whispered Shirl.

Either Coffin did not hear this or had decided
to ignore it. "I called upon your ship, Captain, to
lodge a complaint. A strong complaint. You did
not obtain permission to take one of your boats
for an atmospheric flight. Your officer has been
trying to make excuses for you, telling me that no
copy of port regulations has been received on
board. This excuse I was prepared to accept; after
all, you are strangers here. But I was not told for
what purpose you made your flight."

"I am sure that nothing untoward happened,
pastor," said Steerforth placatingly.

"Then how do you explain this shameless display of nudity—and on, of all days—the Sabbath?
I shall be sending a strong message of complaint
to your owners." He realized his mistake. "A
strong letter of complaint to the Bureau of Interstellar Transport. Meanwhile, any further excur-
sions by your ship's boats are forbidden."

It was useless trying to argue.

"Get on board and get dressed," Grimes ordered the girls. Then, to Coffin, "Rest assured, sir, that I shall remove my obnoxious presence from your world as soon as possible."

He left Steerforth to bear the brunt of the pastor's continued fury as he made his way up the ramp into the ship. Had he stayed he would surely have lost his temper with the man.

Chapter 22

After a while Steerforth joined Grimes in the latter's day cabin. He announced indignantly, "I finally got rid of the sanctimonious old bastard. You certainly didn't help matters by showing up with no less than three girls flaunting their nudity. In fact I'm wondering how I can bring myself to serve under such an unprincipled, atheistical lecher as yourself. Sir."

"I'm sorry," said Grimes, not without sincerity. "But he'd started on you, before I got back, so I let him finish on you. You knew what it was all about. I didn't. Had I stayed I should only have been dipping my oar into unknown waters."

"Into troubled waters," said the chief officer. "Into waters made even more troubled by yourself. And those blasted girls."

The blasted girls made their entrance. Shirl and Darleen were in correct uniform and Seiko was wearing her Madam Butterfly outfit. But either her wig had been replaced by a less formal one or it had been shorn to a page boy bob. With them came Calamity Cassie, ostensibly to make some minor repairs to the small refrigerator in Grimes' bar. ("Are you sure that you want her?" Ms. Scott had asked. "Do you like your beer warm, captain, or having to do without ice cubes?")

"Sit down, everybody," ordered Grimes. "Yes, you too, Seiko. But first of all fetch us drinks."

"And for myself, Captain-san?" asked the robot sweetly.

"If you want one. What do you fancy? Battery acid?"

Cassie laughed. "She'll find none of that aboard this ship. But, believe it or not, there are some archaic wet storage cells over in that apology for a workshop . . ."

Over the drinks Grimes told the story, from his viewpoint, to Steerforth and Cassie. Shirl and Darleen told their almost identical stories. Seiko told her story.

"So, sir," said Steerforth at last, "it seems certain that the silkies can be classified as intelligent beings, even disregarding the claims—which I do not doubt—that Shirl, Darleen and Seiko have been in some sort of telepathic communication with them, there is that gruesome business of their gnawing off people's hands. . . ."

Grimes shuddered. "Gruesome," he said, "is rather too mild a word."

"Could be, sir. But it's a very apposite act of revenge, the sort of revenge that only an intelligent being could conceive." He was warming up to his theme. "What gave us our imagined superiority over certain other intelligent inhabitants of the Home Planet, Earth? The cetacea, I mean. Our hands. Our tool-making, weapon-making, weapon-using hands. With our hands we built the whaling ships, made the harpoons and the harpoon guns. With our hands we launched the harpoons—and continued to do so even after it was generally accepted that the whales are intelligent beings. There was too much money, big money, tied up in the whaling industry for it to be brought to an immediate stop."

"And there's big money tied up in the silkie industry," said Grimes. "Luckily most of it is El Doradan money, and in the Terran corridors of power the El Doradans have at least as many enemies as they have friends. And the silkies have precious few of either. Mphm."

"We . . ." began Shirl, ". . . could be their friends," finished Darleen.

"And I," said Seiko.

"And in any case," said Steerforth, "all of us here are being paid to be the silkies' friends."

"Not enough," complained Grimes, on principle. "And I still don't feel inclined to extend the right hand of friendship to a being who, only a short while back, was going to chew it off."

"But he didn't," said either Shirl or Darleen.

"No thanks to the pair of you," grumbled Grimes ungraciously. "If it hadn't been for Seiko . . ."

"I did only what I had been programmed to do, by your honored father. To look after you," said the automaton in deliberate imitation of the sort of intonation usually employed by not truly intelligent robots, humanoid or not.

Grimes felt that he was being ganged up on by the female members of his crew.

He said, "We can't hang around indefinitely, even though you, Cassie, might be able considerably to delay the progress of the repairs. We have to bring matters to a head, somehow, to engender some sort of situation that will require Federation action . . ."

"But don't forget, sir," pointed out Steerforth, "that *Sister Sue* is not a unit of the Survey Service's fleet, and that only the few of us, gathered here in your day cabin, are commissioned officers of the Survey Service." He smiled briefly at Seiko. "With one exception, of course. But you are, in every way that counts, one of us."

"Should I feel flattered?" she asked.

Steerforth ignored this. "We are not entitled," he went on, "to put the lives of the civilian crew members at risk, any more than we have done already. You're a very skillful saboteuse, Cassie, but even with sabotage accidents can and do happen. I had my fingers crossed during our near-crash landing."

Grimes drew reflectively on his pipe. "What about this?" he asked at last. "Shirl and Darleen—and Seiko—can talk to the silkies. Once a line of communication has been established it's bound to improve. Suppose that the girls are able to persuade the silkies to abandon the rookeries within easy reach, by schooner, of Port Salem and to re-establish themselves on the other side of the planet . . ."

"That, sir," said Steerforth, "would be only a short-term solution to the problem. These local schooners would be quite capable of making long ocean voyages—just as the whalers did on Earth's seas. And as for finding the new rookeries—your old friend Drongo Kane could instruct his captains to use their boats to carry out aerial surveys."

"And people," put in Cassie, "are conservative, no matter where they live, on the land or in the sea. How many villagers, for generation after generation, have continued to live on the slopes of volcanoes, despite warnings and ominous rumblings, even after devastating eruptions? Quite a few, Captain, quite a few. Members of my own family are such villagers." She smiled. "I ran away to Space because I thought I'd be safer."

"You might be," Steerforth told her, "but those of us in the same ship as you very often aren't."

"The rookeries are sacred sites," said Shirl. "They were sacred sites long before the first Earthmen came to New Salem. Even when we, Darleen and I, have full command of the silkies' language we do not think that we shall be able to persuade them to migrate elsewhere."

"You can try," said Grimes. "You might be able to. And if they do migrate it will buy them time and save the lives of possibly hundreds of pups. And by the time that the next season rolls around something else might have turned up."

"As long as you're still around, sir," said Steerforth, "something will. Probably something quite disastrous."

"As long as it's disastrous to the right people," Grimes told him cheerfully.

Chapter 23

Over the years Grimes had come to realize that he was some sort of catalyst; his insertion either by chance or by intent (more and more, of late, by Rear Admiral Damien's intent) into a potentially unstable situation caused things to happen. It hadn't been so bad, he thought, in the old days when he had been as much surprised as anybody at the upheavals of which he had become the center. Then he hadn't led with his chin. Now he was supposed to lead with his chin, and he didn't like it.

That night he was a long time getting to sleep. He relived the threatened, probably fatal mutilation when those grinding teeth were about to close over his wrist. He had faced other perils during his career, but very few during which he had been so absolutely helpless. But now, he consoled himself, the silkies accepted him as a friend. (And Pastor Coffin most certainly did not.)

Once the repairs to the inertial drive had been completed, once the Mannschenn Drive had been recaliberated and once he had stocked up on fresh water he would no longer have any excuse for staying on New Salem. He could tell Calamity Cassie to perpetrate some more gentle sabotage— but, damn it all, this was *his* ship and he just didn't want her damaged any further, and to hell with his Reserve commission and to hell with Admiral Damien.

He thought, *If I'm seen to be hobnobbing with the silkies the good pastor will think even less of me than he does already. Possibly he will take some action against me, do something that will justify my screaming to the Survey Service for protection and redress. After all, legally speaking, I'm no more (and no less) than an honest civilian shipowner and shipmaster going about his lawful occasions, a taxpayer who contributes to the up-keep of the so-called Police Force of the Galaxy.*

He thought of a cover story, of the report that he would have to make if a destroyer were sent to Salem to release Grimes and *Sister Sue* from illegal arrest. *Shortly after my arrival at Port Salem the ruler of the colony, one Pastor Coffin, hinted that I might be interested in taking part in the fur* trade. I was interested—after all, I am in business to make money. And yet I was prey to nagging doubts. I was witness to the brutality involved in the slaughter of the silky pups, the pelts of which are especially valuable. Two of my junior officers, Ms. Kelly and Ms. Byrne, New Alicians, shared my misgivings. (You may be aware that the New Alicians are capable of empathy with all animal life.) Ms. Kelly and Ms. Byrne claimed that the silkies are intelligent beings—just as the cetacea on Earth were finally (and almost too late) found to be. Ms. Kelly and Ms. Byrne were able to communicate with the silkies, using a sort of song language, remarkably similar to that used by the whales in Earth's seas . . .

He thought, That sounds good. I'm wasted in Space. I should be a writer like the Old Man. Mphm. Now we come to the extrapolation. What will Coffin actually do when he finds out that we're on speaking terms with the silkies? What can he do? We haven't much to fear; the only firearms on this planet are those in my own armory. And they'd better stay there. On no account must I appear to be the aggressor. And what if his goons try to rough me up when I'm down on the beach some dark evening, communing with the silkies? (That, of course, is what I want to happen.) Anybody who tries to rough me up when I've my Terrible Trio, Shirl, Darleen and Seiko, with me, will be asking for and getting

trouble . . . I'll have to impress on them that if we
are attacked they are to take defensive action
only . . .

He continued with his scenario. One evening
Ms. Kelly, Ms. Byrne and myself strolled down to
a beach about two kilometers from the spaceport
in a direction away from the city. We were accompanied by my personal robomaid, a very versa-
tile and sophisticated piece of domestic machinery,
one capable of being programmed by her—no,
better make that "its"; sorry Seiko—by its owner
to perform adequately in almost any foreseeable
circumstances. This robomaid is not only waterproof but capable of emitting sounds when completely submerged. Acting on my instructions Ms.
Kelly and Ms. Byrne had programmed the robot
with the silkies' song.

Having arrived at the beach I set up my sonic
recorders and waited, with Ms. Kelly and Ms.
Byrne, while the robomaid waded out into deep
water until lost to sight. Ms. Kelly and Ms. Byrne,
whose hearing is far more acute than mine, told
me that they could hear, faintly, the song that
she—no, it—was singing under the surface. After
a while they said that they could hear the silkies
answering.

Eventually the robomaid emerged from the sea
and walked up on to the beach, followed, almost
immediately, by half a dozen big silkies clumsily
humping themselves up over the wet sand. Ms.

Kelly and Ms. Byrne talked with them by an exchange of musical grunts and snatches of high-pitched song. Now and again Ms. Kelly would interpret for me, telling me that the silkies were pleased that at last humans had come to their world who wished to regard them as friends and not as mindless prey. Through my interpreter I told the silkies that I should do everything within my power to ensure that the fur trade stop.

Finally the silkies lurched back into the sea and Ms. Kelly, Ms. Byrne and I began to walk back to the ship, followed by the robomaid, carrying the recording apparatus. Suddenly men emerged from the bushes that bordered the track. I heard somebody yell, "Dirty silky lovers!" We were attacked, with fists and clubs, with no further warning. Fortunately for ourselves Ms. Kelly and Ms. Byrne possess some expertise in the arts of unarmed combat and, too, the robomaid had been programmed to protect her—no, its—master. Even so we suffered abrasions and contusions. Our clothing was torn. The recorder was smashed. By the time we reached the refuge of the ship we were being followed by a sizeable mob, shouting and throwing rocks. . . .

Grimes didn't like the way that his scenario was progressing. But there would have to be violence before the Survey Service could be called in to take police action, before there could be a full inquiry into the New Salem fur trade. Coffin and his crew would have to be made to show themselves to the universe in their true colors.

He sighed audibly, sat up in bed, switched on the light and then filled and lit his pipe. The sleepless Seiko came in, still in her Japanese guise, carrying a tray with teapot and cup.

She said, "You do not sleep, Captain-san."

He told her, "I am trying to work things out."

She said, "That is the worst of being a self-programming machine." If her flawless face had been capable of showing expression it would have done so. "As I am finding out all the time."

Grimes sipped the hot, soothing tea that she had poured for him.

He said, "Seiko, you're a treasure. I'm not surprised that my mother was jealous of you. . . ."

She said, "It is my delight to serve those whom I love, John."

Normally, had any robot, no matter how intelligent, addressed Grimes by his given name that same automaton would, very promptly, been smacked down to size. But, on this occasion, Grimes felt oddly flattered. He said, however, "You must not call me John in the hearing of my officers, Seiko."

Her tinkling laugh sounded more human than mechanical.

"I know my place, John."

He finished his tea, put down the cup, stretched out in the narrow bed. He complained, "I thought that the drink would make me drowsy but I feel more wide awake than ever. . . ."

She ordered gently, "Turn over."

He did so. She stripped the covers from his naked body. He felt her hands on his back, her smooth, cool, gentle hands, at times firmly stroking, at other times moving over his skin as lightly as feathers. It was like no massage that he had ever experienced but it was effective. A deep drowsiness crept over him. He turned again, composing himself on his left side. Dimly he heard the rustle of discarded clothing.

Surely not . . . he thought.

But it was so, and Seiko slid into his bed, the front of her body fitting snugly to the back of his. She must have actuated some temperature control; her synthetic skin was as warm as that of a human woman would have been. He would have wanted more than she was giving him but knew that, even if possible, it would have been . . . messy.

As he dropped off to sleep he imagined the reactions of his officers should they ever learn—but they never would—that he had gone to bed with his robomaid. He could almost hear the whispers, "The old bastard's actually sleeping with Seiko. . . ."

But, almost without exception, the male members of his crew would be envious rather than censorious. And some of the female ones. And—he actually chuckled—and as for Shirl and Darleen, even at their most vicious Seiko would be more than a match for them.

And Pastor Coffin?

Fuck *him*, thought Grimes just before unconsciousness claimed him.

Chapter 24

The next day Pastor Coffin sent a messenger to the ship. This sullen, black-clad, heavily bearded young man presented Grimes with a sheaf of clumsily printed papers headed PORT REGULATIONS. These Grimes read with interest. There was much repetition. They boiled down, essentially, to a collection of Thou Shalt Nots. The ship's boats were not to be exercised. The ship's crew, of any rank whatsoever, were not to stray from the confines of the spaceport. No materials were to be removed from the spaceport workshop without the written permission of the Pastor. The workshop was not to be used on the Sabbath. And so on, and so on.

The next evening Grimes, with Shirl, Darleen

and Seiko, proceeded to break regulations. There was, he had already ascertained, a guard stationed at the gate to the spaceport area and other guards making their patrols. But these men did not possess the sharp night sight or the super-keen hearing of the two New Alicians and carried, should they feel the need for illumination, only feebly glimmering oil lanterns. Grimes, of course, was equipped with only normal human eyesight and hearing himself so was obliged to rely upon the faculties of his companions.

He and the girls were dressed in black coveralls and shod in soft-soled black shoes. Their faces and hands were coated with a black pigment that, according to Calamity Cassie, who had concocted it from the Odd Gods of the Galaxy knew what, could be removed by a liberal application of soap and hot water. (Grimes hoped that she was right.) Seiko carried a black bag in which the recording equipment had been packed.

The four of them stood in the after airlock, the illumination in which had been extinguished. They watched the bobbing, yellow light that was the lantern carried by a patrolling guard. The man seemed to walk faster as he approached the ship, was almost hurrying as he passed the foot of the ramp. Probably, thought Grimes, he felt some superstitious dread of these impious strangers from the stars. (Coffin, of course, would have told his people what an ungodly bunch Grimes and his crew were.)

"Now," whispered Shirl.

On silent feet she led the way down the gangway with Grimes close behind her, followed by Darleen, with Seiko bringing up the rear. The night was dark, not even the faintest glimmer of starlight penetrating the thick overcast. Grimes had to keep very close to Shirl, sensing her rather than actually seeing her. When she stopped suddenly he banged into her, kept his balance with difficulty. "What . . . ?" he gasped.

"Shhh!" she hissed.

Around the corner of a building came two patrolmen, their lanterns swinging. They were talking quite loudly. "Waste o' time, tha's what. Tell me, man, what we a-doing here, all blessed night? Wha' does *he* think that these ungodly out-worlders are a-going to *do*? Tell me that."

"*He* knows what he's doing, what *he* wants. *He* says that these spacers ain't like t'others, that they're silky-lovers . . ."

"An' they'll come a creepin' out o' their ship in the middle o' the night to love silkies?" The man laughed coarsely. "Let 'em, I say—long's they leave their women so's we can love *them*. Did ye set eyes on their wenches? There's one or two o' them black ones as I'd fancy . . ."

"Watch yer tongue, Joel. That's Godless talk,

an' you know it. The pastor'll not think kindly o' ye should I pass it on . . ."

The voices faded into the distance.

Twice more, before they reached the spaceport periphery, Grimes and his companions had to freeze into immobility, each time warned by the super-keen senses of Shirl and Darleen in ample time. They did not, of course, go out by the main gate but they scaled the fence, high though it was, without difficulty. On the other side there was bushland but not of the impenetrable variety. But by himself, even in broad daylight, Grimes would have become hopelessly lost. He was grateful when, at last, Shirl told him that it would be safe for him to use his pocket torch at low intensity. At least, now, he was not tripping over roots and getting his face slashed by branches. (It was just as well that these bushes were not thorn-bearing.)

Then, surprisingly, they came to a road, the coast road. They crossed it. There was more brush, then there was a beach, and the smell of salt water and the murmur of wavelets breaking on the shore, and a glimmer of pale phosphorescence at the margin of sea and land.

Seiko lowered the big, black bag to the sand, unpacked it, setting up the audio-visual recorder. Then she kicked off her shoes, shrugged out of her coveralls. Her body was palely luminous—and her black face and hands gave her a wildly surrealistic appearance.

She said, "All ready, John."

Grimes said, "Of course, we can't be sure that they will come."

"They will come," said Shirl.

"Sound carries a long way under the water," said Darleen.

Seiko waded into the sea. She was a long time vanishing from sight; here the beach shelved gradually. At last she was gone, completely submerged. Grimes filled and lit his pipe, walked up and down, staring all the time to seaward. On other worlds, he thought, there would be the running lights of coastwise shipping, but not here. And on other worlds there would be lights in the sky and the beat of engines, but not here. Did the Salemites put to sea at night? They must do so, now and again, he decided, but only on fur hunting expeditions to the silky rookeries. And there must be fishermen. There was so much that he did not know about this planet.

"Here she comes," said Shirl.

Here she came, at first only a glimmer of phosphorescence about her neck, her still-black face invisible against the black sea surface. And then there were her pale shoulders, and then her breasts, and her belly, and her thighs ... She was not alone, was being followed up to the beach by six great arrowheads of bio-luminescence, six silkies that disturbed the water only enough to actuate the tiny, light-emitting organisms.

She walked up on to the firm sand. The sea-
beasts wallowed after. Shirl and Darleen greeted
them with musical grunts. The silkies replied.
Grimes, squatting over the apparatus, made sure
that all was being recorded. He envied his companions their gift of tongues. It seemed almost
that those sounds were making sense. There was
emotional content; he was sure of that. There was
wonder, and there was sadness, and a sort of
helpless bitterness.

Then Darleen said, "This is not fair, John. You
are being left out of the conversation. I shall interpret what has been said already."

"Please," said Grimes.

"I speak as a silky," sang rather than said the
girl. "I speak for the silkies. This is our world,
given to us by the Great Being. It is said that,
many ages ago, our wise beings, looking up to the
night sky, reasoned that there were other worlds,
that the lights in the sky were suns, like our sun,
but far and far and very far away. And we—no,
they—felt regret. We should never know the beings
of those other worlds, should never meet them,
should never talk with them in the friendship
that all intelligent beings must feel toward each
other. . . .

"But others preached hope.

"The worlds are many, the sky is vast

"And surely it must come at last

"That friends shall meet and friends shall talk

"And hand in hand in love shall walk . . ."

She laughed, embarrassed. "I am sorry, John; I am no poet. But I tried to translate one of their songs from the olden times. 'Hand in hand in love shall walk' is not, of course, a literal translation—but I had to make it rhyme somehow . . ."

"You're doing fine," said Grimes. "Carry on, Darleen."

"I speak as a silky," continued the girl. "And for the silkies. We swam in our seas, and gathered on the meeting places for communion with our fellows, for the fathering and mothering of our children. We sang our songs and we made new songs, and those that were good were fixed for all time in our memories.

"And then came the ship. . . ." She paused, then said, "There is another song.

"Came the ship and it gave birth

"To the things that walk on earth,

"With their sharp blades that hack and slay,

"That stab and rip and gut and flay . . ."

Shirl interrupted, saying, "I think that we should cut this short, John. Our silky friends are becoming restless; it seems that they must report to their council of elders, which is being held some distance away. And we have to get back to the ship. So I will summarize, without all the poetic language.

"When men, the first colonists, came the silkies were prepared to be friendly. From the sea they watched the strange, land-dwelling beings, decided that they were intelligent like themselves and decided, too, that there were no reasons for hostility between the two races. Men wanted the dry land. So what? They were welcome to it. Even so, they exercised caution. It was quite some time before the first emissaries came lolloping ashore to make contact with the humans, a party of woodsmen who were felling trees to obtain structural timber.

"Some of the humans ran in fear but most did not. The ones who did not run set about the silkies with their great axes. Two silkies out of half a dozen, both of them wounded, made it back to the sea to tell their story.

"But there must have been some misunderstanding, it was decided. There were other attempts at communication—all of them ending disastrously. The silkies decided that the humans just wanted to be left alone. Unfortunately the humans did not leave the silkies alone, although it was not until the start of the fur trade that they became a serious menace. . . ."

And how had the fur trade started? Grimes wondered. Probably some visiting star tramp, whose captain had been given or who had bought a tanned silky skin . . . This curio shown to some friend or business acquaintance of the tramp master, who realized the value of furs of this quality, especially at a time when humanitarians

all over the galaxy were doing their best to ensure
that practically every fur-bearing animal was well
and truly protected . . .

Darleen said, "They ask, can they go now, John?"

"Of course," Grimes told her to tell them.
"Thank them for the information. Let them know
that it will be passed on to rulers far more powerful than the Pastor Coffin, and that these rulers
will take action to protect the silkies. Oh, and say
that I shall want more talks. Ask them if they are
willing."

There was an exchange of grunts.

Then, "Come to this beach at any time," inter-
preted Shirl, "and when the not-flesh-and-blood
woman calls, we shall come."

The silkies returned to the sea and Grimes and
his people commenced their walk back to the
ship.

Chapter 24

Their walk back to the ship was without incident and once over the spaceport fence they were able to elude Coffin's patrols easily. From the after airlock they went straight up to Grimes' quarters where, before they had time to attempt to wash the pigment from their faces and hands, they were joined by Steerforth. The chief officer grinned as he looked at his black-faced captain and Grimes snapped, "Don't say it, Number One. Don't say it."

"Don't say what, sir?" asked Steerforth innocently.

"You were about to make some crack about nigger minstrels, weren't you?"

"Me, sir? Of course not." He leered at the

women. "I was about to say that Shirl and Dar-leen—and you, Seiko—are black but comely." Then he became serious. "How did it go, sir?"

"Very well, Mr. Steerforth. Very well. We got some good tapes. They will be proof, I think, that the silkies are intelligent beings. But you know as well as I do how slowly the tide runs through official channels, especially when there are delib-erately engineered obstructions. And, apart from anything else, it will be months before the tapes get to Admiral Damien—and during that time how many silkies will be slaughtered?"

"So there will have to be an incident," mur-mured Steerforth. "An incident, followed immedi-ately by investigation by the Survey Service."

"And I, of course, shall be at ground zero of this famous incident," grumbled Grimes.

"Of course, sir. Aren't you always?"

"Unfortunately. And now I'm going to get this muck off my face and hands and get some sleep. Goodnight, all of you."

Everybody left him apart from Seiko. It was not the first time that he had shared a shower, but it was the first time that he had done so with a robot. (But he already knew that she was waterproof.)

He slept alone, however.

In the morning he did not join his officers for breakfast but enjoyed this meal, served by Seiko, in his day cabin. Then he sent for the chief officer.

He said, "I suppose that Flo and her gang are already in the workshop?"

"They are, sir."

"I'd like you to wander across some time this morning. Get into a conversation with Cassie—I'm sure that Flo will be happy to dispense with her services. Make sure that you have this mutual ear-bashing where it can be overheard by whatever of Coffin's goons is lurking around to make sure that nothing is damaged or stolen by my engineers. Wonder, out loud, what the old bastard—me—is up to, sneaking out at night with those two cadets and that uppity little bitch of an assistant stewardess . . ."

"Captain-san, I am not an uppity little bitch!" protested Seiko.

But you're an uppity robot, he thought.

He said, "And I'm not an old bastard—at least, not in the legal sense of the word. Anyhow, you get the idea, Mr. Steerforth. Try to convey the impression that I and the ladies are Up To No Good. Nameless orgies out in the bush . . ."

"Can I come with you next time, sir?"

"Somebody has to mind the shop, and it's you. And, in any case, I don't think that you're doing too badly for yourself, from what I've noticed. Aunt Jemima, of late, has been serving *your* favorite dishes at almost every meal."

Steerforth flushed. "Ms. Clay and I have similar tastes, sir."

"Indubitably." Grimes laughed. "But shenan-
nigans, sexual or otherwise, aboard the ship, are
one thing. Shenanigans, especially sexual and indulged in by off-worlders, on the sacred soil of
New Salem, are another thing. You're free to
speculate—and the more wild the speculations
the better. Perhaps on these lines. 'Maybe the old
bastard and his three bitches are having it off
with the silkies. I wouldn't put it past them. I've
always suspected that the four of 'em are as kinky
as all hell.' "

"And are you, sir?"

"Not especially."

"You have a very fertile mind, sir."

"Mphm. It runs in the family, I suppose. Oh,
you might take a pocket recorder with you so that
I can hear a play-back of the way that you'll be
slandering me. It will all be part of the evidence."

"Not to be used against me, I hope, sir."

"If you like," said Grimes, "I'll give you written orders to traduce me."

Steerforth flushed again. "That, sir, will not be
necessary," he said stiffly.

Late that evening Grimes and the three girls, their
hands and faces again blackened, emerged from
the ship. This time the sky was not overcast and
the stars were bright in the sky; even Grimes
experienced little difficulty in finding his way
through the spaceport. As before there were the

patrols, carrying their feeble oil lanterns. As be-fore these were easily—too easily? wondered Grimes—eluded. The fence was scaled. Beyond it was the almost familiar bushland. It seemed to Grimes that the same path through it was being followed as before.

Suddenly Shirl whispered in his ear, "Stop here for a little while, John. Pretend to be lighting your pipe. . . ."

"Why pretend?" he muttered, pulling the foul thing from his pocket.

They stood there while Grimes went through his usual ritual.

"Yes," murmured Darleen. "As I thought. . . ."

". . . we are being followed . . ." continued Shirl.

Somewhere behind them a twig cracked.

Grimes finished lighting his pipe.

"One man only . . ." breathed Darleen into his ear.

Grimes took his time over his smoke. *Let the bastard wait,* he thought, *not daring to make another move until we move on.*

Finally, "All right. Let's get the show on the road," he said in a normal voice.

He knocked out his pipe on the ground, stamped on the last faintly glowing embers to extinguish them. He moved off, letting Shirl take the lead. Darleen followed close behind him and Seiko brought up the rear. They came to the coast road, crossed it. They emerged on to the beach. The recording apparatus was set up on its tripod. Seiko divested herself of her clothing. Shirl and Darleen followed suit, one of them saying, "Let us have a swim first. What about you, John?"

He said, "The water's too bloody cold."

(If there was to be any confrontation he would prefer to be fully clothed.)

Shirl pressed herself against him in what must have looked like an amorous embrace. She whispered, "We might as well give the bastard an eyeful."

"The three of you can," he whispered back.

Seiko, her body palely luminous in the starlight, waded into the sea. The wavelets broke about her legs, her body, flashing phosphorescently. Shirl and Darleen followed her, flinging themselves full length as soon as there was enough depth. They sported exuberantly. It was as though they were swimming in a sea of liquid diamonds. "Come on in!" one of them called. "The water's fine!"

"Too cold for me!" Grimes shouted back—but if it had not been for that unseen watcher he would have joined them.

Finally they tired of their games and came wading into the beach. Droplets of slowly fading phosphorescence fell from their nipples, gleamed in their pubic hair. One did not have to be kinky, thought Grimes, to appreciate such a show. He wondered if *he* was appreciating it. No doubt his eyes were popping with wonderment, sinful lust and holy indignation.

"We should have brought towels," said Darleen practically, attempting to dry herself with her coverall.

"It is time that Seiko finished singing her song," said Shirl.

And now Seiko emerged from the sea, fully as beautiful as the two New Alicians, adorned as they had been by living jewels of cold fire. The silkies followed her, up on to the beach, grunting musically, and each of them was wearing a coat of radiant color. Grimes wondered how he could ever have thought them ugly.

"They bid you greeting, John," sang Shirl.

"Tell them that I am pleased to see them," replied Grimes.

What followed came as a surprise to him. He had been expecting a conversation—a conference? —such as the one in which he had taken part the previous night. But this was more of an orgy. The women—and Seiko was one of them—seemed to be determined to put on a show for Coffin's spy. Grimes sat there, his pipe for once forgotten, watching in wonderment. The naked human bodies— although one was human only in form—entertwined with the darkly furred bodies of the sea beasts ... The caresses, the musical murmurings ... (These tapes, thought Grimes, who had his prudish moments, he would not be submitting to any higher authority back on Earth, he would not be showing to Steerforth back aboard the ship.) Pale female flesh sprawled over rich, dark fur . . . Flippers that caressed breasts and thighs with what he would have thought was impossible gentleness. . . .

And at the finish Seiko standing there, on a low, sea-rounded rock, while, one by one, the silkies each gently placed a flipper on her bare feet before sliding away, down into the sea. It seemed like (was it? could it be?) an act of obeisance, of worship even.

Grimes, his prominent ears still burning with embarrassment, filled and lit his pipe. He demanded, "What . . . " then fell silent.

"It is all right, John," Seiko told him. "We are alone again. He, the pastor's spy, is gone. Along the coast road. I am surprised that you did not hear him. He was not very cautious. Anyhow, you can talk without being overheard."

"I did not hear him," snapped Grimes. "There were too many other things to listen to. And watch. Just what, in the name of all the Odd Gods of the Galaxy, were the three of you up to?"

"You said that you wished to shock Pastor Coffin's people, John," Shirl told him.

"I didn't say that *I* wanted to be shocked. The worst of it was that the three of you seemed to be enjoying it."

"And why should we not?" asked Darleen

sweetly. "Have you ever experienced the feel of soft, rich fur against your naked skin? And we learned, on your world, that many human women are not above enjoying sexual relations with their so-called pets, their cats and their dogs and the like."

"That's different!" almost shouted Grimes.

"How so, John?" asked Shirl. "Oh, all right. Those pets, on Earth, are not intelligent by human standards. The silkies are intelligent. Unfortunately, as far as we and they are concerned, our bodies are too . . . different."

"That will do," snapped Grimes. "Get dressed. And remember this, if Coffin's man has reported to his master, and if the patrolmen try to arrest us, the three of you are to use only such force as is required to prevent our capture. I want an incident, not a massacre. But I don't want to spend what's left of the night in Coffin's jail."

But he had no real fears of this latter. He already knew of the fighting capabilities of Shirl and Darleen and strongly suspected that Seiko, by herself, would be more than a match for a small army, provided that this army did not deploy nuclear weaponry.

Nonetheless they made their way back to the ship without incident.

Grimes told Steerforth a somewhat edited version of the night's doings.

Chapter 25

So the bait had been noticed. Would Pastor Coffin bite? Grimes had little doubt he would do so, and no doubt at all that the pastor would find Shirl, Darleen and Seiko an impossibly hard mouthful to swallow. As long as there was an incident, as long as Grimes could scream that he and his people, respectable, law-abiding merchant spacepersons, had been assaulted by the Salemites there would be an excuse for Survey Service intervention. Damien had half-promised that the destroyer *Pollux* would be loafing around in the vicinity of New Salem, doing something or other, during the period of Grimes' stay on the planet.

After spending a rather lazy day Grimes and the three girls emerged from the ship under the

cover of darkness and followed their usual route
to the beach. It was another brightly starlit night
but this time they were not followed. When Grimes
got himself entangled in a particularly tenacious
bush he envied the pastor's men. They—assuming
that they would be at the shore to watch the
horrid goings-on—would have made their way to
the beach by the coast road.

They were waiting there. Grimes, by himself,
would not have been aware of their presence but
Shirl and Darleen, with their super-sharp hearing,
were.

"Do we do the same as last night, John?" whispered Shirl.

"No," said Grimes firmly. (Tonight's audio-visual
tapes would have to be produced as evidence at
the inquiry into the almost inevitable incident.)
"No. Just a meeting, a conference with the silkies."

"But can't we have a swim, even?" asked
Darleen.

"All right, all right. Have your swim." (There
was very few worlds—although Salem was one of
them—where the spectacle of attractive naked
women splashing in the sea would evoke so much
as a raised eyebrow.)

Grimes set up the recorder. Seiko stripped and
waded out into the water, deeper and deeper,
until she was lost to sight. Shirl and Darleen got
out of their coveralls, ran down to the sea, fell
full length and began striking out in a sparkling

flurry of phosphorescence. Grimes lit his pipe.
He thought that he heard a faint rustling in the
bushes inland from the beach but could not be
sure. He was far from being afraid but was beginning to feel distinctly uneasy.

Shirl and Darleen emerged from the water, joined
him where he sat. Shirl produced a packet of
cigarillos from a pocket in her coveralls. Both
girls lit up. Neither made any attempt to get
dressed. Grimes remarked upon this.

"The air is quite warm," said Shirl. "We shall
let it dry us."

"Last night," said Darleen, "we were very uncomfortable when we put on our clothes over wet
skins."

"Suit yourself," said Grimes.

And why should he be the only one dressed?
Because all that was happening was being recorded, that was why. Because friends as well as
enemies in the Survey Service would laugh themselves sick when, at the inquiry, the tapes were
played, with an audio-visual recording of Grimes
enjoying a roll in the hay (or a roll on the sand)
with two of his junior officers. Too, why should
he give those unseen watchers an even better
show than the one that they were already enjoying?

Seiko waded out from the sea, dripping phosphorescence. She was followed by six big silkies.
The same ones as the previous night? Grimes

couldn't tell. Apart from differences in size and pelt coloration they all looked the same to him.

The sea-beasts disposed themselves in a semicircle, facing the humans and the pseudo-human and the audio-visual recorder. They talked and sang, and Shirl, Darleen and Seiko replied to them in kind. Now and again Shirl would interpret for Grimes' benefit.

The silkies wanted just one thing, to be left alone. They admitted that not all humans were as bad, from their viewpoint, as the colonists. They admitted that exchanges of knowledge and of information might be advantageous but, essentially, they had very good reason not to trust humans.

"Not even you, John," said Shirl sadly. "We—Darleen and myself and Seiko—have been prepared to cast aside the artificial trappings of so-called civilization. You have not. We have made naked contact with the silkies. You have not. And you did not approve, in your heart of hearts, when we did. . . ."

"I'm keeping my trousers on," growled Grimes. "Tonight especially."

At last the conference was over. Again Seiko stood on that sea-rounded rock; again the silkies made their obeisance, one by one gently placing a flipper on her slim feet. Then they were gone, back into the sea.

The three women began to get into their coveralls—and from the bushes, armed with staves and clubs, poured Coffin's men.

The women were caught at a disadvantage, half into and half out of their coveralls. Too, at first, they paid overmuch heed to Grimes' admonition not to fight back too viciously. And Seiko, upon whom Grimes had been relying, was one of the first casualties. The butt of a long stave struck her fair and square upon her vulnerable navel, where her ON/OFF switch was situated. She did not freeze into complete immobility—the switch had not been fully actuated—but thereafter was able to struggle only feebly. By this time both Shirl and Darleen had been struck about their heads with heavy clubs, as had been Grimes himself. After that he had only confused recollections of the struggle. He was flung violently to the sand, face down, and got his mouth and his eyes full of grit. A heavy boot on the small of his back pinned him in this supine position. His wrists were yanked up and back, pulled together by rough rope that broke the skin. Despite his kicking his ankles were bound.

He heard Coffin's voice, an unpleasant combination of smugness and harshness.

"We have them. The witch and her three disciples."

"But one of them is the outworld captain, pastor."

"It matters not. Captains may still be sinners and blasphemers, worshippers of false gods. His rank—such as it is—matters not. He will stand trial with the witch and the two shameless trollops."

Grimes felt hands lifting him. He was dropped on to a hard wooden surface. His nose began to bleed. Somebody was dropped beside him, and then two other bodies on top of him. He heard the squeaking of not-very-well greased axles and felt the jolts as the unsprung vehicle, whatever it was, was pulled (by manpower, he supposed) along the rough coast road. He managed to lift and to turn his head so that his painfully bruised nose was no longer in contact with the floorboards.

He could speak now, although it required a great effort.

"Seiko . . ."

"Yes . . ." her voice came at last, weak, barely audible.

"You're the strongest of us. Can you break your bonds?"

"No . . . I have . . . lost . . . my strength. They . . . hit me. You know . . . where."

"You should not have told us not to fight back," said Shirl.

"Where . . . are they taking us?" asked Darleen.

To hell in a handcart, thought Grimes but did not say it.

"What will they do to us?" asked Shirl.

"Throw us into jail, I suppose," said Grimes. "But not to worry. Mr. Steerforth will bail us out." (*And how much will that cost?* he wondered, the mercenary side of him coming to the surface.)

Chapter 26

They were not thrown in jail.

They were dragged roughly out of the four-wheeled cart and securely bound, with iron chains, to four upright posts, also of iron. Dazedly Grimes looked about him. He and the others had been brought to the open area between the waterfront, with its jetties, and the town. He was facing a long table, on which were three oil lanterns, at which were sitting Pastor Coffin and, one to either side of him, two clerkly men. Other lanterns were hung from tall posts, illuminating the faces of the crowd that had turned up to. . . . To see the fun?

Coffin glared at Grimes from beneath his heavy, black brows. He demanded, in a deep voice, "Prisoner at the bar, how plead ye?"

Grimes mustered enough saliva to wash most of the sand and blood out of his mouth. He spat, regretting as he did so that the pastor was out of range. He spat again.

"Prisoner at the bar, how plead ye?" repeated Coffin.

"I do not plead," almost shouted Grimes. "I demand. I demand that I and my people be returned, at once, to our ship!"

"Prisoner at the bar, how plead ye? Guilty or not guilty?"

"Guilty of fucking *what?*" demanded Grimes, considering that this occasion called for some deliberate obscenity in his speech, realizing, too late, that his words could be misconstrued. (But, he thought, *he* had not played an active part in that orgy.)

Coffin seemed to be losing his patience. "John Grimes, you will answer my questions. Are you, or are you not, guilty of witchcraft?"

"Witchcraft? You must be joking."

"This is no joking matter, Grimes. Are you guilty or not guilty?"

"Not guilty."

One of the clerkly men was writing in a big book with an antique-looking pen.

"Your plea has been recorded," said Coffin. He turned his attention to Shirl. "You, woman. How do you plead?"

"Not guilty," she replied in a firm voice.

"And you, woman. How do you plead?"

"Not guilty," said Darleen.

"And . . . you?" Coffin was glaring at Seiko, who was sagging in her bonds.

The robot was speaking with difficulty. "Not . . ." she got out at last. "Not . . . guilty."

"Very well," said Coffin. "Now we shall hear the truth. Clerk of the court, call the first witness."

The man sitting on his right—not, as Grimes had been expecting, the man writing in the book—rose to his feet, called, in a high voice, "Matthew Ling, stand forward! Matthew Ling, stand forward!"

A burly fellow shouldered his way through the crowd, took his stance between the prisoners and Coffin's table.

"Matthew Ling, identify yourself," ordered the pastor.

"My name is Matthew Ling," said the man. "I hold the rank of Law Enforcer Second Class."

"Tell your story, Law Enforcer Ling."

"May it please the court," said Ling, "my story is as follows." He spoke as do police officers all over the galaxy when giving evidence, his voice toneless. "Pursuant to information received and to the instructions of Pastor Coffin I followed the four accused from the spaceport to Short Bay. At first I thought that they were members of the Negro race; as the court is aware there are some of those accursed people in the crew of the starship. I caught glimpses of their faces while

they were still on the spaceport grounds, and saw
that they were black . . ."

"As their faces," said Coffin, "are black now.
And their hands. That alone is damning evidence.
Why should a God-fearing man or woman blacken
the Lord's handiwork as evinced on his person? I
will tell you. As a badge of submission to the
Prince of Darkness. But continue, Law Enforcer."

"May it please the court . . . I followed the
accused through the bush, across the coast road,
and then concealed myself in the bushes, in a
position overlooking the beach at Short Bay. I
watched the accused setting up a device on a
tripod, a devil's machine of some kind that emit-
ted colored lights. Then the male accused sat
down on the sand and began to inhale the poison-
ous fumes of some weed that he was burning in
the bowl of a small implement. While he was
partaking of his noxious drug the three female
accused disrobed. I saw then that their faces and
hands were blackened but not the rest of their
bodies. The female accused then disported themselves in a wanton manner before the male accused.

"The three female accused waded into the sea.
Two of them swam, with unnatural skill. The
third one, the one with the black hair, waded out
into deep water until she was lost to sight. At no
time did she swim or attempt to swim. The other
ones returned to the beach and, still naked, sat

beside the male accused, joining him in the ritual inhalation of some noxious weed.

"Finally the black-haired female accused came up from the sea, followed by six silkies. What happened then I should never have believed unless I had witnessed it with my own eyes. The three witch-women sported with the silkies. It was a scene of sickening bestiality." (At last there was a hint of emotion in the flat voice.) "But even the witches and the silkies tired of their lewd games. The silkies returned to the sea. But the black-haired witch stood on a rock, and each silky, before going back to the sea, made a sign of submission to her by placing its flipper on her bare feet. I had seen enough and made my way back to the city, by the coast road, to make my report."

"And what you have told us is the truth," stated rather than asked Pastor Coffin.

"It is, sir," said Ling.

"Objection!" shouted Grimes.

Coffin consulted with the two clerks then said, "John Grimes, it pleases us to hear your objection. Say your say."

"Your Law Enforcer Ling is not a reliable witness, pastor."

"Indeed? How not so?"

"Law Enforcer Ling stated that on the night in question I sat down on the beach to enjoy a quiet smoke. That is correct. He also stated that Ms Kelly and Ms Byrne, after they had finished their swim, also enjoyed a smoke. They did not. That was because they had brought no smoking materials with them."

Ling was called to the pastor's table, was engaged in a low-voiced conference with Coffin and the other two. Finally he stood aside.

The pastor said, "It is your word, John Grimes, against the word of my law enforcer. . . ."

"My word," said Grimes hotly, "and the words of two of my officers."

"There may," admitted Coffin magnanimously, "be some confusion in Law Enforcer Ling's memory. For this there is ample excuse. What he witnessed would have been enough to turn the mind of any man not of exceptionally strong and pious character. And Law Enforcer Ling was with me tonight, when you and the other accused were apprehended. I saw, with my own eyes, both you and the women Kelly and Byrne indulging in your filthy habit. The objection that you have raised is a mere quibble."

Grimes subsided. *They can't shoot us for smoking,* he thought. *Not even on this bloody planet.*
But for witchcraft?

"Call the second witness," ordered Coffin.

"Job Gardiner," called the clerk. "Job Gardiner. Stand forward!"

"My name is Job Gardiner," said the man, who could almost have been twin brother to Matthew Ling. "I hold the rank of Chief Law Enforcer . . ."

He cleared his throat. "Persuant to information received and to direct orders from Pastor Coffin, I, together with a party of law enforcers—among whom was Matthew Ling—made my way to Short Beach by the coast road. Pastor Coffin accompanied us, saying, and rightly, that this was a very serious matter and that he would have to exercise overall command of the operation. . . ."

And so it went on.

". . . it was obvious, to the pastor and myself, to all of us that the four accused were talking to the silkies and that the silkies were talking to them. And such things cannot be. Then the silkies returned to the sea, but before they did so they made bestial obeisance to the black-haired witch. The pastor ordered us to arrest the four blasphemous outworlders. We did so, and we smashed the Devil's machine that they had brought with them."

But the tapes should have survived, thought Grimes The tapes, and their damning evidence. But would they be retrieved? Would they ever be played back?

"The court has heard the evidence," said Coffin. "We all have heard the evidence. It is obvious that at least one of the accused, the black-haired woman, is a witch. It is probable that the man and the other two women are lesser witches, or acolytes. But we must be sure before we order our law to take its course. Chief Law Enforcer Gardiner, I order you to apply the acid test."

"Law Enforcer Ling," ordered Gardiner in his turn, "bring the acid."

Coffin smiled bleakly at Grimes. "We have our methods, outworlder, of determining the guilt or otherwise of witches. The acid test is one of the more effective. An accused witch is required to drink a draught of acid. If he or she is uninjured, then obviously he or she is a witch and is dealt with accordingly. If he or she suffers harm, then he or she is possibly not a witch."

"Heads I win, tails you lose," said Grimes.

"You speak in riddles, Grimes. And nothing you say is of any consequence."

Ling returned from wherever he had gone carrying a large bottle. He handed this to his superior, then went to stand behind Seiko, pulling her head back with one hand, forcing her mouth open with the other. Gardiner, who was now wearing heavy gloves, approached her from in front. He raised the unstoppered bottle, began to pour its contents between her parted lips. Some of the corrosive fluid spilled on to Seiko's clothing, which smoked acridly.

There was a murmur from the crowd, more than a murmur, a chorus of shouts. "She is a witch! Kill her! Kill her!"

Then, abruptly, Seiko regurgitated the acid that had been poured into her. The burning stream struck Gardiner full in the face. He dropped the bottle, which shattered, and screamed shrilly, clawing at his ruined eyes.

Incongruously the robot murmured, "I . . . am . . . sorry. But my . . . circuits . . . were not . . . designed to . . . take such punishment . . ."

Grimes was not sorry. The Chief Law Enforcer had deserved what he got. (To how many flesh-and-blood women had he applied this acid test?) And the bottle was broken and, hopefully, it would take some time to fetch a new one and, meanwhile, anything might happen . . .

Grimes hoped.

Chapter 27

The whimpering Gardiner was led away by two of his subordinates. Presumably whoever passed for a doctor in this town would be able to assuage the pain, although not to do anything to save the man's eyesight. But that was the least of Grimes' worries. His main concern was for Seiko, for Shirl and Darleen and for himself. He reproached himself for not having carried to the beach, in addition to the recorder, a portable transceiver so that, at all times, he would have been in communication with his ship.

But he had never dreamed that Coffin would go to the extremes to which he already had gone— and to what extremes was he yet to go? *And you, Grimes, of all people,* he told himself, *should*

*have learned by this time that allegedly civilized
people are capable of anything, no matter how
barbarous.*

Coffin was speaking. "There is no doubt that
the woman is a witch. Not only has she survived
her ordeal uninjured but she has severely injured
my chief law enforcer. She must pay the penalty."
He paused judicially, turned his head to stare at
Grimes, Shirl and Darleen. "It was my intention
to order that the acid test be applied to the other
three accused. Unfortunately no further supply of
acid is readily available. So I shall, therefore,
temper justice with mercy. Grimes, Kelly and
Byrne will be given the opportunity to confess
and to recant. Should they do so, their ends will
be swift and merciful. Should they not do so,
they shall be executed in the same manner as
their mistress. They will be permitted to watch
her sufferings and, hopefully, such spectacle will be
a stimulus to their consciences.

"Bring the faggots!"

Men and women brought bundles of sticks.
(These must, thought Grimes, have been prepared
well in advance.) They piled them around the
stake to which Seiko was chained, concealing the
lower half of her body. A law enforcer poured
some fluid—flammable oil, it was—over the faggots. He struck a long match, applied the flame
all around the base of the pile.

With a loud *whoosh* the oil ignited and there

was an uprush of smoky fire. Seiko's hair—but *it's only a wig*, thought Grimes—flared and crackled. Then the initial fury of the burning oil subsided but the faggots had caught, were snapping in the heat, emitting sparks, sending their flames curling up around Seiko's body. Although the cloth of her coveralls was flame resistant it was beginning to char and to powder. A sigh, a horribly obscene sound, went up from the mob as one perfect breast was exposed.

Suddenly, audible even over the crackling of the fire, the murmurs of the crowd, there was a startlingly loud *click!* Seiko, who had been sagging in her bonds, stood erect. Her wrists, which had been tied behind her back, were already free, the flames having burned away the rope. But even if this had not been the case it would not have mattered. The strength that she now exerted to snap the chains would have been more than enough to break mere vegetable fiber. As she stood there, ridding herself of the last of her bonds, the crumbling remnants of her clothing fell from around her smoke-smudged body. She was like, thought Grimes, Aphrodite rising from the sea—a sea of fire. And he, even at this moment, had to repress a giggle. A Venus without arms, a Venus de Milo, he might accept—but a bald-headed one was altogether too much. (Her body paint had survived the fire although her wig had not.) Even so, she was beautiful—and not only because her escape from the pyre had brought a renewal of hope.

Men were shouting, women and children were screaming, but none dare approach this vengeful she-devil. Coffin was bellowing, "Seize her! Seize her! Strike her down!"

"Good on yer, Seiko!" yelled Darleen. "Show the bastards!"

There was a meter of broken chain in Seiko's right hand. She threw it. It wrapped itself around Coffin's neck, all but decapitating him. His two clerks squealed in terror, dived under the table, from the surface of which the pastor's blood dripped down upon them. Seiko stepped out of the fire, flames and sparks splashing about her feet. Two law enforcers, braver or more stupid than their fellows, ran at her with heavy clubs upraised. She countered their assault with the *savate* technique that she must have learned from Shirl and Darleen; her long right leg flashed out while she pivoted on her left heel; first one man and then the other (although there was almost no interval between the two blows) was the recipient of a crippling kick to the groin. In horror Grimes noted that the trousers of each unfortunate were smouldering where the kicks had landed. Seiko's feet must be almost redhot. (But it was her feet for which he felt concern, not the genitals of the law enforcers.)

He felt the heat emanating from her body as she

approached him, as her hands reached out for his chains. But she was careful not to touch him.

She said, "Do not worry about *me*, John. I am heat resistant. I feel no pain, as you know it. And it was the heat of the fire that released my master switch . . ."

She left him to his own devices, went to free the two New Alicians.

Grimes looked around, fearing fresh attack. But the light of the oil lanterns on their posts revealed a waterfront empty save for himself and his women, the body of Coffin sprawled over the table and the two still-living (but for how long?) bodies of the law enforcers. The pair of clerks had made their escape unnoticed.

"Well," said Grimes with deliberate matter-of-factness, "that seems to be it. We've had our incident. Let's get back to the ship. Come, Shirl. Come, Darleen. And you, Seiko, can guard our rear."

"I am staying," said the robot.

"Seiko, I order you to come with us."

"John, your father was my original owner. He ordered me to protect you when necessary."

"Then protect me as I walk back to the spaceport."

She said, "We could be attacked." With a long forefinger she touched her navel. "I have learned my vulnerability in a scrimmage. A club, a flung stone, even a heavy fist and I can be jolted into near-immobility. There is only one way to ensure your safety. Those people . . ." she gestured toward the town, ". . . must be taught a lesson."

But it was not toward the houses she ran but to the slipway, up which the schooners were hauled for the scraping and caulking of the underwater portions of their hulls. It was toward the slipway that she ran, and down the slipway. When her body entered the black water there was an uprising of steam.

Then she was gone from sight.

"Crazy robot!" grumbled Grimes. "Being cooked must have affected her brain . . ."

"She knows what she is doing, John," said Darleen loyally.

"Does she? I wish that I did." He could sense that from darkened windows he was being watched. He wondered how long it would be before the New Salemites, seeing that the most dangerous witch had plunged into the sea, would come pouring out of their houses to exact vengeance for the death of their pastor and the injuries inflicted upon his law enforcers. He said, "I think that we should be getting out of here."

Shirl said, "But we can't leave Seiko . . ."

"I know," said Grimes. "But . . ."

"Do you *hear* her?" Shirl asked Darleen.

"Yes." Then, to Grimes, "Do not worry so, John. Everything will be all right."

From whose viewpoint? he wondered.

Then up the shipway she strode. The sea had washed the grime of smoke and fire from her pale body. Up the slipway she strode—and behind her, a living tide, surged the silkies. As she passed Grimes on her way inshore she made a gesture that was more formal salute than cheery wave. And the silkies grunted—in greeting or talking among themselves? But Shirl and Darleen replied in kind.

The robot and her army reached the sea frontage of the town. There was shouting and screaming, the splintering crashes as doors were burst in, as wooden walls succumbed to the onslaught of tons of angry flesh and blood. Fires started in a dozen places—the result of overturned lamps or lit by intent? Grimes did not know but suspected that Seiko was exacting retaliation in kind for what she had undergone. Fires started, and spread.

"This has gone too far," said Grimes.

"It has not gone far enough," Shirl told him. "The silkies said to us that she had told them that they were not to kill. To destroy only, but not to kill. That's the trouble with robots. They have this built-in, altogether absurd directive that human beings are never to be harmed by them."

"Wherever did you get that idea?" asked Grimes.

"While we were waiting for you on Earth we did quite a lot of reading. There were some books, classics, by an old writer called Asimov."

"Then what about *him*?" Grimes gestured toward the pastor's body. "Wasn't *he* harmed? Fatally, at that."

"Yes, John," said Darleen patiently. "But he was going to harm you, and Seiko was doing her best to protect you."

The town was ablaze now, the roaring of the flames drowning out all other noises coming from that direction. Satisfied with the havoc that they had wrought, the silkies were returning to the sea. There was light enough for Grimes to see that some were wounded, with great patches of fur burned from their bodies. Others bled from long and deep gashes. But their musical grunting sounded like a chant of victory.

Seiko brought up the rear. Again her body was smoke-blackened. She approached Grimes and bowed formally. "Captain-san, it is over. We spared the church and a large hall adjacent, and the people are huddled in these buildings, praying."

"How many killed?" demanded Grimes.

"Nobody by intent, although two or three may have died accidentally. But we let them seek refuge in their houses of worship and I refrained from applying the torch to these."

"You did well," said Grimes at last. "All right. The sooner we're back on board the ship the better."

"I am sorry, John," Seiko told him. "I cannot accompany you."

"That's an order, damn it!"

"Which I cannot accept. I was built to serve, John, as well you know. But you do not really need me. They . . ." she gestured toward the sea, to the silky heads, their eyes gleaming with reflected firelight, that were turned inland, looking at the humans and the robot. "They need me, much more than you do."

"She is right," said Shirl and Darleen as one.

Above the roar of the burning town, beating down from the sky, was the arrhythmic clatter of a small craft's inertial drive. One of *Sister Sue's* lifeboats made a heavy landing not far from where Grimes was still trying to argue with the women. From it jumped Steerforth and Calamity Cassie, each with a laser pistol in hand.

"You're all right, Captain?" demanded the chief officer. "We saw the flames and thought that we'd better take action."

"You did right," said Grimes. "And now you can get us back to where we belong."

"Good-bye, Harald," said Seiko. "Good-bye, Cassie. Tell the others good-bye for me."

She was, Grimes noticed, holding her right hand protectively over her navel.

"We can't leave you here, Seiko," objected Steerforth.

"She can look after herself," said Grimes harshly. "And, in any case, it'll be days yet before *Sister Sue* is capable of lifting off. If—no, *when*—you change your mind, Seiko, you'll know where to find us."

The boat, with Steerforth at the controls, clattered upward. The chief officer made a circuit of the seaport area before setting course for the spaceport. New fires had broken out; alongside their jetties the schooners were ablaze.

She was thorough, was Seiko, thought Grimes. Very thorough. It would be a long time before, if ever, there was another silky hunt on New Salem.

All that next day he was expecting her to come walking back up the ramp, into the ship. And the day after, and the day after that . . .

Chapter 28

The mess was well on the way to being cleaned up.

The destroyer *Pollux* had been within range of *Sister Sue*'s Carlotti radio, even though the signals had been broadcast and not beamed. She had dropped down to the spaceport, with Grimes usurping the functions of New Salem Aerospace Control. (Presumably the lady who usually did the talking to incoming traffic was still huddled in the church with her badly frightened fellow colonists.)

Her captain, Commander Beavis, had served under Grimes many years ago and was cooperative. Damien must have told him that Grimes was once again, although secretly, an officer of the Federation Survey Service, senior to Beavis. That gentleman managed to imply that Grimes could issue orders rather than mere suggestions. But appearances were maintained for the benefit of the crews of both ships. Grimes was the innocent shipmaster whose life, and the lives of certain of his officers, had been threatened by the people of this world. Beavis was the galactic policeman who had come hurrying to the rescue.

Beavis had the people and the equipment to be able to do something about the plight of the colonists, whose city had been almost entirely destroyed. He set up a sizeable township of tents, complete with field kitchens and a hospital. He interrogated various officials and recorded their stories. Then, aboard *Sister Sue*, he heard Grimes' report and watched and listened to the playback of the various tapes—one of them heavily edited—including that final one, which had been recovered, undamaged, from the beach. He interviewed Shirl and Darleen and Steerforth and Cassie.

Then when he was alone with Grimes, relaxing over a drink, he said, "I shall put all this material in Admiral Damien's hands as soon as possible, sir. He's going to love it—and so will Madame Duvalier. I rather think, somehow, that the New Salemites are going to be resettled—preferably on some world with no animal life whatsoever. . . ."

"If they could find some way of harvesting plants really brutally they'd do it," said Grimes.

"In spite of all that's happened they still regard themselves as the Almighty-created Lords of Creation. And, more and more, I'm coming to the opinion that any life, all life, should be treated with respect and compassion."

"Even robots, sir?" asked Beavis with deceptive innocence.

Grimes laughed. "All right, all right. There was that bloody tin messiah, Mr. Adam, years ago. He got what was coming to him; I wasn't sorry then and I'm not sorry now."

"I was thinking of Seiko, sir."

"Mphm."

"She would pass for a very attractive woman. You must miss her, sir."

"I suppose I do," admitted Grimes. "But she'll be back. She'll know when I'm due to lift. She'll be back."

At last the repairs were finished and the fresh water tank refilled. All that remained to be done was the recalibration of Sister Sue's Mannschenn Drive. While this was being carried out only a skeleton crew would remain on board—Grimes himself in the control room, Flo Scott in the inertial drive room and, of course, all the Mannschenn Drive engineers in their own compartment, making their abstruse calculations and arcane adjustments. The theory of it was that if anything should go wrong, if the ship fell down a crack in the

Space-Time Continuum, the captain and his top-ranking technicians might—just might—be able to get her back to where and when she belonged. Ships—only a very few ships but ships nonetheless—had been known to vanish during the recalibration procedure. Of that very few an even smaller number had come back, and not to the planets from which they had made their unscheduled departures. Sometimes, after only a very short absence from the normal universe, their crews had aged many years. Sometimes, during an absence of years, only minutes had elapsed for the personnel. Some crews claimed to have met God; others told horrifying stories of their narrow escapes from the clutches of the Devil. Grimes, good agnostic that he was, did not believe such tales, saying, if his opinion were asked, that it is a well known fact that the temporal precession fields engendered by the Drive have an hallucinatory effect upon the human mind.

Recalibration, to him, was a process similar to old-fashioned navel gunnery, the procedure known as bracketing. Under ... Up ... Over ... Down ... still Under ... Up ... Right on! Salvoes!

So he sat in *Sister Sue*'s control room, smoking his pipe, waiting for Daniel Grey, the Chief Manschenn Drive Engineer, to start doing his thing. He looked out through a viewport, saw his people, together with a number of Beavis's officers, standing by the stern of *Pollux*, watching. Grey's voice came from the intercom speaker, "All ready, Captain."

"Thank you, Mr. Grey. Commence recalibration."

He heard—and felt—the deep hum as the rotors of the Drive commenced to spin, a hum that rapidly rose in pitch to a thin, high whine with an odd warbling quality. Outside the scene changed. *Pollux* was no longer there. Neither were the spaceport administration buildings. The planet was as it had been before the coming of man. *Under,* thought Grimes. The scene changed again. There were only ruins of buildings, barely recognizable as such under the growth of bushes and small trees.

Over.

Then *under* again, with a few rough shacks to mark where the spaceport proper would one day be.

Over. . . .

The familiar buildings were there, but showing signs of dilapidation. Grimes got up from his seat, looked down through the port at the concrete apron. It was cracked in many places, with weeds thrusting through the fissures. He went down from the control room to his quarters. There was an odd unfamiliarity about them. Who was the auburn-haired woman whose holographic portrait was on the bulkhead behind the desk in his day cabin? It wasn't Maggie, although there was a certain similarity. In his bedroom he took his uniform cap from the wardrobe, looked into the mirror to adjust it to the right angle. With fast dissipating puzzlement he noted the strange cap badge above the gold-braided peak, a rather ornate winged wheel, and the single broad gold band, the insignia of a commodore, on each of his shoulderboards. Passing through his day room he flicked a good-humoured salute at the portrait of Sonya.

He took the elevator down to the after airlock, walked down the ramp to the cracked and scarred concrete. His first lieutenant, Lieutenant Commander Cummings, saluted smartly. Grimes returned the salute. He said, "I'm taking a morning stroll, Commander Cummings. To the old seaport."

"Shouldn't an armed party be going with you, sir? After all, according to the data, the natives aren't overly friendly towards visitors."

"I've been here before, Commander. And the ones who most certainly were not friendly were the human colonists. And, as you know, they were resettled."

"As you please, sir. But . . ."

"I shall be all right, Commander."

You always are, you old bastard, he could almost hear the officer thinking.

And—*old bastard*? he thought. Yes, he was getting old. Not in mind, not even in body, but in years and experience.

The road from the spaceport to the seaport,

along which he had first walked so many years ago, was still passable. Nonetheless he began to wish that he had taken one of the ship's boats instead of making the journey by foot. At any age at all he did not enjoy having to force his way through bushes. Although the sunlight was not especially hot he had worked up a good sweat by the time that he got to what had been Salem City. The charred ruins were not yet completely overgrown and the church and the hall, in which the colonists had taken refuge, were still standing.

Like rotting fangs the jetties still protruded into the sullen sea, from which projected, at crazy angles, the fire-blackened spars that had been the masts and yards of the schooners.

The slipway, still in a good state of repair, was almost as he remembered it.

And up it walked Seiko.

She was as she had been when he first saw her, in his parents' home. The transparent, glassy skin had been cleaned of all vestiges of body paint and beneath it glittered the beautiful intricacy of that non-functional yet busy clockwork. Her well-shaped head was bare of the last trace of hair. But something had been added, one item of clothing. She wore a broad belt of gleaming metal mesh with a golden buckle—more shield than buckle—that covered her navel.

She bowed formally. "Captain-san."

He bowed in return. "Seiko-san."

She said, "This is Liberty Hall. You can spit on the mat and call the cat a bastard."

He laughed and said, "You haven't lost your sense of humor."

"Why should I have done so, John? The silkies are not a humorless people."

She looked intently at his cap badge, the braid on his shoulders.

Grimes asked, "What's puzzling you?"

She said, "Your ship is the same. I saw her coming down. But your uniform is different."

Grimes told her, "She is no longer my ship. Oh, I command her, but I no longer own her. And her name has been changed. She is now *Faraway Quest*, the survey vessel of the Rim Worlds Confederacy, in whose naval reserve I hold the rank of commodore."

"And all the people I knew, when she was *Sister Sue* and you were owner as well as captain?"

"They have all gone their various ways, Seiko."

"I would have liked to have met Shirl and Darleen again . . ."

"I still hear from them, about once a standard year. Eventually they returned to their home planet, New Alice."

"When next you write, please give them my regards."

"I shall do so."

"And when next you are on your home planet,

John, please give my regards to your respected parents."

Grimes told her, regretfully, "They are both long gone."

"Then will you, for me, make obeisance at their tomb and pour a libation?"

"I shall do that," promised Grimes.

The pair of them fell silent, looking at each other, a little sadly. It was a companionable silence.

Grimes broke it. He said, "You can have your old job back, if you want it."

She replied, "Thank you. But the silkies still need me. I am their hands and their voice. I speak for them to the occasional visitors to this world, human and nonhuman. Were I not here there would be acts of aggression and exploitation."

"So that's the way of it," said Grimes.

"That is the way of it," she agreed. Surprisingly she took him in her strong arms, affectionately pressed him to her resilient body. Grimes did not resist. She released him. "Good-bye, John. You must return to your ship. To your ship. We may meet again—I hope that we do. We may not. But always, always, the best of luck."

She turned away from him, walked down the slipway to the sea, an almost impossibly graceful, glittering figure. It seemed to Grimes that the silkies had been waiting for her. There was a great flurry of spray as she entered the water, a chorus of musical gruntings.

And then she and they were gone, and Grimes started his walk back to the ship, cursing the spiky bushes on the overgrown road that seemed to be determined to hold him prisoner on this planet.

He was sitting in his chair in the control room. The Drive had been recalibrated. All hands had returned on board, had proceeded to their lift-off stations. Steerforth looked curiously at Grimes' forearms, bare under the short-sleeved uniform shirt, at his knees, bare under the hem of his shorts.

"Those scratches, sir. . . . How did you get them? You look as though you've been in a cat fight."

"Do I?" said Grimes coldly. Then, "All right, Number One. Let's get the show on the road."

Steerforth said, "But couldn't we wait a little, sir? What about Seiko? Couldn't we send Shirl and Darleen down to the sea to try to do some submarine singing to call her back? After all, they're rather special cobbers of hers."

"We shall be happy to try," said Shirl.

"Make it lift off stations, Mr Steerforth," ordered Grimes.

"But Seiko . . ."

"She'll be all right," said Grimes, with convincing certainty.

DAW

PHILIP K. DICK

"The greatest American novelist of the second half of the 20th Century."

— *Norman Spinrad*

"A genius . . . He writes it the way he sees it and it is the quality, the clarity of his Vision that makes him great."
— *Thomas M. Disch*

"The most consistently brilliant science fiction writer in the world."

— *John Brunner*

PHILIP K. DICK

In print again, in DAW Books' special memorial editions:

- [ ] **WE CAN BUILD YOU** (#UE1793—$2.50)
- [ ] **THE THREE STIGMATA OF PALMER ELDRITCH**
  (#UE1810—$2.50)
- [ ] **A MAZE OF DEATH** (#UE1830—$2.50)
- [ ] **UBIK** (#UE1859—$2.50)
- [ ] **DEUS IRAE** (#UE1887—$2.95)
- [ ] **NOW WAIT FOR LAST YEAR** (#UE1654—$2.50)
- [ ] **FLOW MY TEARS, THE POLICEMAN SAID** (#UE1969—$2.50)
- [ ] **A SCANNERS DARKLY** (#UE1923—$2.50)

DAW

DAW BRINGS YOU THESE BESTSELLERS BY
MARION ZIMMER BRADLEY

☐	CITY OF SORCERY	UE1962—$3.50
☐	DARKOVER LANDFALL	UE1906—$2.50
☐	THE SPELL SWORD	UE1891—$2.25
☐	THE HERITAGE OF HASTUR	UE1967—$3.50
☐	THE SHATTERED CHAIN	UE1961—$3.50
☐	THE FORBIDDEN TOWER	UE1894—$3.50
☐	STORMQUEEN!	UE1951—$3.50
☐	TWO TO CONQUER	UE1876—$2.95
☐	SHARRA'S EXILE	UE1988—$3.95
☐	HAWKMISTRESS	UE1958—$3.50
☐	THENDARA HOUSE	UE1857—$3.50
☐	HUNTERS OF THE RED MOON	UE1968—$2.50
☐	THE SURVIVORS	UE1861—$2.95

Anthologies

☐	THE KEEPER'S PRICE	UE1931—$2.50
☐	SWORD OF CHAOS	UE1722—$2.95
☐	SWORD AND SORCERESS	UE1928—$2.95

NEW AMERICAN LIBRARY
P.O. Box 999, Bergenfield, New Jersey 07621

Please send me the DAW Books I have checked above. I am enclosing
$_____ (check or money order—no currency or C.O.D.'s).
Please include the list price plus $1.00 per order to cover handling
costs.

Name _____

Address _____

City _____ State _____ Zip Code _____
Allow 4-6 weeks for delivery